THE BECKONING SERIES:
ELURA

By A.J. Watts

Order this book online at www.trafford.com
or email orders@trafford.com

Most Trafford titles are also available at major online book retailers.

Printed in the United States of America.

ISBN: 978-1-4269-8762-5 (sc)
ISBN: 978-1-4269-8819-6 (e)

Library of Congress Control Number: 2011913101

Trafford rev. 08/01/2011

 www.trafford.com

North America & international
toll-free: 1 888 232 4444 (USA & Canada)
phone: 250 383 6864 ♦ fax: 812 355 4082

For

Tom (Maynard) Thompson

CHAPTER ONE

It was a hot day in June and the kids on the bus are complaining of the weather, and talks of what their summer was going to be like. School has ended for the next three months, which was what the excitement was about. The bus began to pull away from the curb taking its normal route and was soon letting kids off at their stops.

As Tommy sat in his seat alone like he usually did was not paying attention to what the other kids were talking about, but was wondering what the summer holds for him. Never having expectations about anything; after the death of his parents, who were killed by an explosion inside of the house? He can't understand why they were killed and he was not, after all he was also inside the house when it happened. He came, out of the fire unharmed except for his clothes which were burnt off of him. No cuts on him were found on his body. It has been six months since the accident; he was considered a miracle lucky to be alive. Was called a freak; by other kids.

With his backpack on his lap, Tommy opened the pencil pocket and brought out a newspaper clipping which he had cut out of the school library. He had unfolded the clipping and read the headlines "TWO KILLED IN BIZZARD EXPLOSION" below the headline the reporter continued to write about the incident, neither the police nor the fire department had any glue as to what happened there was no evidence of how the explosion had ignited. Furthermore the reporter goes on about how Tommy survived without a scratch on him. As he finished reading the clipping he carefully folded back up and put it in the backpack zipping up the pencil pocket he then began to look out the window waiting for his stop to come. His thoughts raced back to the time of the explosion trying to remember what his parents look like. Every day it gets harder and harder to remember them.

The bus stopped and Tommy got off. He waited for the bus to go by so he can cross to the other side of the street. He looked both ways before running across then slowdown he began to walk to the third house a colonial style with four pillars to help support the porch roof. Walking up to the door he pulled his key from his jeans to let himself in slamming the door he bounded up to the second floor. With his head down he did not see his foster mother there until he looked to open the closet door.

"Hi," he said as he put the backpack away in the closet.

Miss. Mason it blond headed with blue eyes and a figure that only a model supposed to have. Tommy always thought that's what she should be doing and not becoming a foster parent. She stood up after putting clean clothes into the drawers and closes them.

"Well you're back early?" She ruffled his hair as she passed him on her way out. Tommy rolled his eyes up into its head even though she couldn't see him do it.

"It's the last day; I'm supposed to leave early"

"That's right, I totally forgot about that." Looking down at him sheepishly as they entered the kitchen. [See what happens when you do too much work Mason, you forget things.] She thought as she looked through the fridge to find something to fix for the both of them. "So how was it?" she asked taking items out for their sandwiches.

"It was ok I guess, any better than yesterday. 'Cause I know that I won't have to go back to school until September." Taking a seat at the table and was watching her work.

"What are your plans for the summer?" Mason asked as she took up a knife and started to cut the sandwich in half then she stopped to look at him for a reply.

"Don't know?" Looked down at his hands as he began to play with the salt shaker. "I can hang around here with you until I have to go back to school."

"What's wrong?" She finished up cutting the sandwich taking it to the table with a glass of milk. "C'mon you can tell me." She gave him an encouraging smile.

"Well it's that I can't seem to make any friends around here everybody thinks I'm a little too weird because of what happened to me that's all." Sounding depressed he puts his head between his hands.

"Tommy there are a lot of kids around here who won't know what you have been through, losing your parents is a hard thing to forget. Just because you survived the accident does not mean you're weird." Sitting across from him she took both of his hands away from his face as she folded her hands around his he looked up from the table to face her. "They're scared just as you are in wanting to be your friend. Most people are just plain shy." Squeezing his hand to reassure him as the tears started down his face he looked away from her.

"Then why didn't they come up and asks me if I wanted to play with them. When I went to one of them to ask if he wanted to play freeze tag, or play on the playground. You know what he said to me… GET AWAY FROM ME YOU FREAK!!! The other kids laughed at me and kept on calling me freak, FREAK!" Tommy shot up from the table shouting the word over and over until the door of his bedroom slammed.

Sitting there at the table Mason was horrified to hear what Tommy had said to her. Anger began to take a hold of her as she cleaned the table off of the unwanted sandwich and putting into the fridge. Mason thought about what to do about the problem. After she had finished cleaning she knew what had to be done and it was to call Louise Bishop Tommy's social worker and knowing what will happen if she did. She did not know how he would feel about moving to another home. Knowing all too well she will not be able to help him and take care of him for she was behind on her mortgage about to lose the house anyway because she can not afford it. She stood up and starts toward the stairs reaching his room she knocked but was not waiting for an answer letting her self in.

"Tommy, there is something I have to tell you, before I talk with Ms. Bishop." He sat up.

"What is it?" Looking at her a moment then he cast his eyes down to the bed thinking that he was going to get it for the outbursts of anger in the kitchen. Mason moved inside the room and sat on the edge of the bed. Trying to find the words to tell him what he should not have to hear, she promised herself that she would always tell him the truth of was going on. Deciding whether or not to say anything about it, she turned to face him.

"You know that I would never do anything to hurt you right?" his puffy eyes met hers.

"Yeah I know that." He gave her a weak smile.

Mason moved closer to him.

"Well what's going on is that I'll have to move from this house because I can't afford to keep up the payments. So what I have to do is to talk to Ms. Bishop about placing you in another home, I am wondering how you feel about that."

"Did I do something wrong?" tears came down his face again "I'll be good I don't want to be going to another home and into an area that I don't know." He got off the bed and started out of the room Mason quickly caught him turning him around she got down on our knees so that his eyes was leveled with hers so she can talk to him not as a mother but as a friend.

"Don't ever say that. That's the thing you're not the cause of this mess. Tommy life is not always sad and unhappy. You'll feel happy again and will live your life as a regular kid with hopes and dreams to fulfill. You just have to go on and never give up trying." She gently pulled him to her not letting go; Mason began to cry she didn't want to let Tommy go out of her life for she had broken one of the many rules of being a foster parent which is to love him as if he was her own son. From the very start when she first saw him she knew that he was special. For six months the love she had given him grew, at times when he would wake up screaming from a nightmare covered in sweat she would be there to softly tell him that everything would be all right. Mason has always felt his pain during those times. Tommy's head was in her lap for he fell asleep from exhaustion stroking his light brown hair and thinking of a way to keep Tommy and yet still move. She would have to talk to Louise about the possibilities. As she shifted her weight around Tommy woke up sitting up he yawned and looked to Mason.

"How long was I asleep?" was stretching his arms.

"A half an hour to an hour it's hard to tell." Mason picked the sleep from his eyes then slowly got from the floor for she felt that numbness in her legs, so she sat down on the bed for a few minutes. "Do you want something to eat now?"

"No I don't feel like eating at all." Taking one of Mason's hands and helping are up from the bed as the both went down to the living room. Tommy entered first and sat down on the couch which faced the front storm window. Looking out into the yard thinking how unfair life is and wishing that he would not have to worry about where he will be sent to next. Wondering if what Mason said was true, about life been happy again he'll just have to see for himself. Feeling like life just ended he got up from the couch and went to the window the day dreaming of another place far from the present moment. Mason not saying anything got up from her chair and left the room. Entering a hallway she went to the phone and picked up the receiver she dialed Louise Bishop's number.

Tommy was still looking out the window when she finished the conversation with Louise to confirm what was going on and if there was a way to place him with a permanent family. It was an uneasy conversation from the start because Louise was having a bad time trying to get parents to see Tommy. She has found one couple who liked him from the picture and had made arrangements for him to see them the next day. Mason came in and stood by him; He snapped back to the real world.

"So, what are you thinking about?" watching him stare out the window appearing to be in deep thought.

"Oh, nothing much just wondering what would be like for me. You know expectations things like that. What bothers me the most is that I feel as if I'm an object that someone owns instead of a human being for someone to love?" Mason was listening to him and knowing that he was about to the end of his rope and does not know who to trust any more. This is a lot for a ten year old boy to hold in him.

"You've just got to hang in there okay. I spoke with Ms. Bishop and there's a couple who want to take you out to have some fun how does that sound to you?" hoping the news will lift his spirit up and out of the depression state.

"Really"

"Yep, they will be here in the morning to pick you up." She Smiled.

"That's great, who are they?" he looks to her for more information.

"Well their last name is Benson that's all I know on that." She looked at her watch. "I've got things to go get from the store. You want to come with me?"

"I'll stay here if it is okay? I don't feel like doing much except taking a walk."

"Sure, you just be careful." She said while checking to see if she had everything. Then she left the house by the front door. Tommy watched her drive off before closing it and locking the door, going around to the side of the house where he kept his bike. Walking into the sidewalk he got on it and pedaled down Martin Ave. Passing the ocean view park he continued down four more blocks then he turned left on Cedar Street in half a mile up time began to slow down when he approached Washington Place turning into the street he looked around the neighborhood where he had lived six months ago before his life took a drastic turn. Suddenly he stopped, when he saw the burnt remains of the house he used to live in. He still can't figure out how or why it happened. Getting off his bike he walks it towards the driveway, and drops it letting it hit the pavement not bothering to put up the kick stand. For he felt drawn to the house for some reason soon he found himself in the middle of the ruins of what used to be the kitchen. Tommy kept on walking through until the painful memories surfaced in his mind. Finding the surroundings has changed back to the night of the explosion. He was standing in the living room and saw the furniture materialize out of thin air. Looking around he saw everything in its place just as he remembered it.

"Who's that handsome young man?" Tommy quickly turned around to find his mother dressed in an evening gown for the New Year's party. She was looking beautiful with her long brown hair hanging from the shoulders and blue eyes which goes perfectly with her dress. The very face that Tommy thought he had lost forever was now standing in front of him.

"Mom, is that you?" not believing his eyes.

"Yes it's me. Who did you think I was?" standing there with their hands on hips.

"At first I thought you were Mason." Feeling cold he wrapped his arms around himself, as if the blood had ran cold in his veins.

"Are you all right?" She looks concerned about his well being she came closer to him put her hand on his forehead to see if he has a fever. "Your white as a sheet Tommy, are you okay?"

"I think so, I just feel like I woke up from the terrible nightmare." He said has the feeling of her hand warmed him.

"So what was a nightmare about?" Concern left her face.

"I dreamed that you and dad were killed an explosion in this house and I was the only one who survived, then after that it got worse." Feeling the need to hug her he puts his arms around her waist.

"We're not going to die; we will be here until we are old and gray." She kissed him on the forehead.

"This dream was so real mom." His father came into the living room cutting them off.

"Honey, I can't seem to get this tie together would you do it for me please?" As she was tying the bow tie his father mumbled to himself something about not having to work the next day. When she had finished he looked down at Tommy and ruffled his hair like he used too. "Hey sport," Giving him a hug and not wanting to let go and smelling his dad's favorite aftershave. All the memories of fun times they had together came back to him as if it was yesterday. "We got to finish getting ready for the party okay." His father returned the hug and letting go and he did the same going to his room he laid down. Suddenly there was a piercing scream coming from the living room. He quickly jumped from the bed and ran into the living room to see what was happening. When he entered there was a blue light coming from the window and he heard the deep humming it was making. Things on the shelves fell off and glass breaking as it hit the floor as the humming shook the house. His father came in to see what was going on, seeing the look of horror on his face everything was as if it was right out of a movie as the blue light changed to red the beam had hit his mother in the chest and exited out her back. Seeing his mother fall to the floor he screamed but nothing came out, he tried to move from the doorway but found that he could not because he was frighten another red beam appeared out of the window hitting his father in the arm as he cried out in pain, holding is arm he watched in horror as he heard his fathers last words.

"OH MY GOD, THEY HAVE FOUND US, THEY HAVE FOUND US!" Another red beam caught him in the head and fell over and died. Tommy was scared and crying for his life when a beam was coming towards him, as it hit him in the chest knocking him off his feet and he slams into the wall behind him. Everything went black, nothing but cold darkness. His surrounding came back in to focus; he saw that he was standing in the same spot during the time he was knocked against the wall by a beam of red light. Sweat trickled down his chin as he began to be aware of what just happened to him. He knew that deep down inside him self a part of his mind had woke up from a long sleep. Tommy remembers what went on the night of the explosion, which 'was no accident at all. Who ever killed his parents also thinks he is dead as well. When they find out he's still alive they will come back for him. He thought it through and knew that who ever they are had more than one chance to finish the job therefore he was in no danger.

Pondering his father's last words he turned to leave the burnt remains of what once was his home, was not looking where he was going and tripped over some of the churned wood. His arms went out away from his body to try and brace himself. Hitting the ground arms first, Tommy let out a painful cry. Bringing him self slowly to a sitting position and waited for the pain to past, he then examined both of his arms saw that he had only skinned them brought them down to his side. All the anguish and frustrations began to come out in tears feeling and wishing there was something he could do to change all that has happened. Sitting for a few more minutes to let the pain in his arms stop throbbing. He started to get up slowly being careful not to fall again. He was almost to a standing point when he saw something glittering in the late afternoon sun. The light was reflecting off a shinning object. Taking a half step he bent down to pick up the object; suddenly recognizing the medallion, which he always wore around his neck ever since he was a baby. His mother told him it was a family heirloom it was very special and he should never take it off. She would not tell him anymore just that he will find out when the time comes.

The medallion was still on the chain and looks like it was brand new. No damage was done to it during the explosion. Holding the medallion closer to his face, so he can get a better look at the markings he had seen before. Finding it very interesting he looked and saw two circles inside a large sun with a star which almost looks like a person in between the circles. The first was a milky blue color and the other was red. As he stood there staring at the medallion so entranced by its markings he did not realize how late in the day it was. The next door neighbor came out of his house, he was about to water the lawn with the hose, seeing Tommy in the middle of the rubble.

"Hey boy, get out of there before you get hurt!" The man yelled giving scaring him running to his bike he peddled up the street as fast as he could. He came in knowing well he was late. Feeling his pockets making sure that it was not a dream; feeling the cool circler medallion rubbing his leg as he entered the kitchen. He saw Mason at the counter cutting carrots like mad.

"Hello, I'm back from my bike ride?" He said as he headed for the fridge.

"So where did you go?" She dumped the carrots in the bowl.

"Oh, I went to the park to see what kind of fun they had over there." Hoping she wouldn't catch him in a lie.

"You've been gone for three hours." She said looking to see him with his head still in the fridge.

Tommy had closed the refrigerator door and turned around to give her an explanation for his being late. "I lost track of time, sorry."

"Make sure it doesn't happen again alright." Sounding tiered from the work she had done that day. All Mason wanted to do was to relax for the rest of the evening after dinner. As they were having dinner nothing was said between the two of them. Tommy finished eating he excused him self from the dinner table and went up stairs to his room for bed. He was tired from the day of emotional stress and for the memory of what really went on the night of his parent's death. He laid there in bed thinking what he should do next. Feeling that everything is falling apart and there is nothing he can do to stop it from happening. Looking outside the window at the sky which was turning darker, he watched the stars twinkle out. Forgetting his problems for the moment as he laid there watching the twilight sky. Hoping to see a shooting star will pass before he falls asleep. Sleep began to take a hold of his eyes he could no longer hold them open and had closed. Rest came to take him away from his waking nightmares, suddenly a streak of fire had gone across the sky then it disappears towards the earth. Tommy's adventure is about to begun.....

CHAPTER TWO

Alan Tate was working late that night finishing up his report from the usual traffic accidents. Sitting over his desk writing the last of the report of the day signing his name he picked up the papers and placed them in the file box on the corner of his desk. Reaching for a requisition form to start on, he could hear what was going on in the front office where the night receptionist was arguing with another woman who was pleading with her to see someone. The night receptionist was telling her that there was no one who can help her at the time but to come back in the morning during regular office hours, hearing this Alan Tate got up from his desk and went to the front of the station, entering he looked at Margret who was the front office worker.

"I didn't know you were here deputy." She looked down at her work, to avoid anymore embarrassment.

"Hi, I'm deputy Tate is there anything I can do for you?" He stood there looking at her for she was very appealing to him and did not notice a boy standing behind her with very scared eyes.

"It's not me deputy, it's the boy." She sighed before telling him. "Well, I was driving home from work and it was dark so I didn't think about putting on the bright lights so I hit something and it was him." She put her hand on the boy to comfort him.

"You mean you saw the boy in the road and almost hit him with the car?" He said trying to make sense of what she was saying.

"Yes, that is what I've been trying to tell you." Bring up a hand to rub away the pain in her forehead.

He bent down to the boy's level. "Hey, kid what is your name?"

"He doesn't talk; I have been asking him about where he lives and he just points to the sky." The woman said.

"Did you already check his clothes to see if his name on it?" He asked.

"No I didn't I just brought him here. Look the child is obviously afraid or in shock from the experience he just had. Is there anything you can do for him?" She looked at him with hopeful eyes.

"There is a place where we can put him until his parents claim him that is if they do, which I don't think they will." shaking his head sadly.

"Well, what happens if they don't come for him?"

"He will belong to the state. You also got to understand that even if his parents do return they will be charged with child abandonment." Looking at the boy and then started to check to see if there was a name on his clothing. "Either way he would end up in a foster home or put up for an adoption." Tate stood up after searching the back of the boy's shirt and pants with no luck in finding a name. "Come on back here I have a place where you can take him to, the name is Mason Hollenbeck she likes to be called by her first name though." Walking up to his desk he reached for a sucker and gave it to the boy, then got the rolodex out of one of the drawers. Sitting down in the chair Tate thumbed through the cards finding what he was looking for took a piece of paper and wrote the address down for the woman. "Here you go." He gave her a piece of paper.

"Is there other kids there?" She said while reading the address.

"Well as far as I know there is only one kid there and his name is Tommy. He lost his parents in a fire six months ago; he never plays with other kids because of what happened to him." Sitting back in his chair, he crossed his arms.

"Yeah, I've read it in the newspaper. But it is a shame he has to go through all this alone. She stood there frowning. The boy was looking at the sucker as if he didn't know what it was stuck it in his pocket. Reaching into his shirt he pulled out the medallion walks over to Tate and showed it to him.

"May I see it?" Asking the boy for permission the boy nods his head. Tate took a closer look; he saw a green background and what looks like a city in the middle of the medallion. Flipping it over to see what was on the back and found nothing there. "Here you go sport." Letting the medallion fall back on the boy's chest, who smiled for the first time that night? Standing up, all of them left the back office and returned to the front office area.

"So deputy, are you going to charge me with reckless driving?" She said as they were turned the corner of the hallway which leads straight into the front reception area.

"No, just make sure you have your bright lights on at night okay." He said turning to leave but stopped and twirled back around, seeing them at the door. "By the way miss, what is your name?" She turned to answer his question.

"Oh, how rude of me; my name is Faith McCray." Her face was burning red with embarrassment as she told him.

"Keep me informed okay, I care what happens to him." Tate smiled at her for the redness of her face makes her more attractive than she already was.

"I'll do that." Faith and the boy left the station to the address Tate had given her.

Tate went back into the office area to tidy up his desk for the next afternoon shift. He has been on the force for eight years and was married to a wonderful woman who was proud to be his wife. Until one day there was a robbery at the local supermarket. Tate was called in as a back up for the police dept. He managed to slip in through the receiving doors where new produce is brought into the store. He looked down each row to see if any one was hurt. Then he began to make his way to the front of the store. When Tate approached him he made it known that he was a cop, sent to take the girl's place which the robber was holding on to for dear life. The robber was looking at Tate intently trying to figure out how he got in since he checked all the entrances to make sure no one could get in or out. Taking the necessary precautions so the girl wouldn't be shot, Tate did what the robber told him to do. He took out his gun and laid it on the floor then sliding it to the robber with his foot. Tate then started up a conversation with him trying to see what he wanted exchange for the girl. The robber, who was looking in all directions to see if anyone was going to catch him off guard, didn't like small talk with a cop knowing that he was just buying sometime for the police to figure out way into the store. The man's face began to sweat, he knew that the guy is about to make a move and that he has to be ready for anything. The robber was sure of one thing; he wasn't going to get caught by the police. He threw the girl towards Tate who fell back into the snack stand in front of the check out line. As he fell over and landed on the floor, he saw the robber draw up his gun to shoot. There was a scream as Tate broke the girl's fall and then there was the shots being fired one after the other. When the robber had finished the round he dropped the gun and ran. Tate had his eyes closed during the time, for no one had taken a shot at him before. As Tate got up from the ground he had checked himself for bullet holes then had bent down to pick up the girl and also checked her and found nothing on her as well. The mother of the girl raced to hug her daughter. As he saw some people gathered around at the checkout line were he had fallen, walking over and seeing his wife lying dead on the ground he started pulling people away getting on his knees and held her in his arms for the last time.

Snapping out of his memories he sat at his desk and looking at his watch to see what time it was. He finished clearing his desk off and putting the last of the reports in the filing tray. Tate stood up and slipped into his jacket hearing Robert Loudon talking to Margret in the front office. Opening the top drawer of his desk and retrieved his keys. When Tate was about to leave for the night the phone ranged on the desk, picking up the receiver. "Hello, Deputy Tate here."

"Deputy, this is Faith McCray I took the boy over to the foster home, and talked with Miss Mason. She wanted to know what the boy's name was, so I named him Kevin until we find out his real name. We also talked about Tommy who is still trying to put his life back together after the death of his parents. The poor kid has no friends no family he just keeps to him self."

"I know how he feels." Tate said as he pushes his thoughts of his late wife out of his mind. "I was there that night when he just walked right out of the flames, how a boy could survive an explosion and his parent died. It doesn't make any since at all."

"What do you mean?" Tate looked up to see Loudon entering the room.

"Do you still have my card?"

"Yes, but" He cut her quickly.

"Great call me at home in an hour, okay."

"Okay, talk to you then bye." Faith hung up and there was silence.

Tate hung up his end of the line putting the receiver back on the hook and turned to make sure everything was in order for his shift the next day. He turned to leave.

"Who was on the phone?" Loudon was saying as he put a check mark on the in column next to his name.

"It was a personal call, if you don't mind." Tate was getting angry for Loudon always tries to make everything his business. When things don't go his way he makes it miserable for everyone who are trying to do there job.

"I only asked." He said innocently.

"Well don't, one of these days your curiosity is going to get you killed.'

"Yeah right" He scorned. "At least I'm not the only one whose curious these days. Believe me."

"What! Are you referring to me?" He looked at Loudon, who's ready to start a fight. Loudon looks up from his phone messages that he had received before coming on shift.

"No, I meant people in general." saying it in a low tone of voice.

"That's what I thought you meant." Tate knew very well he was talking about him but decided to let it go this time. He was not in the mood for a fight. Although in the past Loudon had pushed him too hard and he took a swung at him hitting him in the face. After that Tate was suspended for a week. This is one of those times Loudon knows when to start on him. Putting his keys in his pocket Tate left the station before he makes another comment about him.

Faith was sat up in her living room reading a book when she looked up and saw what time it was, laying her book down on the end table getting up to get a closer look at the clock seeing it was quarter past ten and it was nine o'clock when she last called Alan Tate at the sheriffs station. Hoping he would be up at this hour. Strolling towards the bedroom she sat on the bed, picking up the phone she dialed his number.

"Hello," the voice on the other line answered.

"Is Deputy Tate in?" Faith said, unsure of whom it was.

"This is he, Faith is that you?

"Yes, it's me. You wanted to call back on your home number." Kicking off her shoes she curled up on the bed.

"I've been waiting for you to call so I can finish the conversation without any interruptions."

"Okay, what I want to know is how Tommy can just get up and walk out of a house after it had exploded." She felt awkward about the situation.

"That part of the story is still unexplainable. But the part of no one hearing or even feeling the impact of the explosion is what amazes me." He said as he tried to contain his excitement about the whole thing.

"You mean no one heard or felt the impact of the blast?" She couldn't believe what was being said.

"Yep, here is the worst part about the whole story. The police and the sheriff's department decided to close the case without an investigation. That was supposed to be done regardless what the case maybe."

"So what is your theory about why they didn't investigate?"

"Well, at first I thought it was because of too many loose ends, I came to find out that it wasn't the case at all."

"Well, what was it?" Faith began to really listen as he began to tell her how he found out that the report was never filed and how his co worker Loudon shows up every time he went to the burnt house to look for clues to find out what really happened. Later on Tate was going through Loudon's desk and found report after report of missing persons, traffic accidents are the ones he has. He explained to her that the reports were to be filed on a computer so to be worked on later. He also told her about Loudon's ambitions to get ahead of the competition for sheriff next year.

"Isn't there anything you can do to let the Sheriff know what he is up to? I mean without Loudon knowing what you are up to?"

"No not yet, I want to find out things about him first before I go to Sheriff Wilson about it because I am going to have proof to back up my story."

"So do you think that Tommy's case was accidental?" Faith asked him.

"With what evidence I have to go on I have to say no, because no one saw or heard the explosion that someone was trying to kill all of them for some reason or another and is yet to be explored." Tate said on the other end of the line while Faith was hearing the clinging of pots and pans being dragged out of the cupboard and onto the stove.

"Well deputy, I am going to turn in for the night but I would like to know more of what you uncover about the case. Although 1 know that it is not open, so be careful okay."

"I will and Faith you can call me Alan okay."

"Sure good night Alan."

"Good night Faith." Tate hung up the phone and prepared himself something to eat then went into the bedroom to read a book. He did not want to go to sleep for he knew that he would dream the nightmare all over again and he was not up to waking up in cold sweat. So he got into bed and picked up the book he started reading where he had left off from the night before soon after he started he began to drift off to sleep into a dreamless sleep.

Faith sat on the bed after putting the receiver on the hook again. Wondering if there would be anything she could do to help Alan in the search for the truth to a mystery that is slowly opening up. She finally decided to do just that. Taking a pen and paper she began to right down possibilities to look into. When she had finished there was a knock on the door. Getting up from the bed she went to the door and opened it. Seeing no one on the other side of the door she started to close it when she looked down to the door mat there sat a shiny metal box which seems to radiate different colors she bent down to pick it up with care and went into the house. Closing the door behind her she went to the kitchen table and sat down, wondering whether or not to open it. Getting up Faith went to the cordless phone and dialed Alan's number again. Tate picked it up on the third ring.

"Hello," he said in a sleepy voice.

"Hi Alan, it's me again. You know after we had finished our conversation over the phone I got a knock at the door just a few minutes ago and when I went to see who it was there was no one there except a box that is very unusual looking and I was going to open it but I thought it may contain something important. I was wondering if you wouldn't mind coming over and take a look with me. This is weird I was not expecting anything at this late hour, so would you be able to come, I know you are tired.

"I will be there in a few." He hung up.

Faith was still sitting in front of the box examining it and notice symbols engraved into the box on the front and on the sides. She knew that she had seen nothing like it anywhere. Putting the box down on the table she got up to fix a pot of coffee before Alan arrives. The door bell has rung its chimes as she was in the kitchen fixing a late night snack. She took the tray with her into the dinning room sitting the tray down on the table and hurried to the door to let her guest in. "Come on in." Stepping aside so he can enter then quickly closed the door behind him.

"So what's this about a box being found on your door step?*

"It's on the dinning room table. I had examined it and I never seen any thing like it. Also the engraved symbols are some kind of language from another place I think." As they moved towards the table Alan picked up the box to see what she was talking about, he too had no idea where the box came from.

"Did you open the box yet?" He continued to look at the box in wonder what was inside.

"No because I wanted to wait until you got here."

"Well let's get it opened." Both of them sat there as Alan lifted the lid of the box. Finding a note written in hasty hand writing, taking it out Alan read it out loud to Faith. PLEASE WEAR THESE THEY WILL PROTECT YOU ON YOUR JOURNEY. Putting aside the note, he reached inside and brought out two medallions that are alike and similar to the one Kevin has. But the difference is that the two Alan held in his hand were both totally blue.

"What the hell" were the only words he could find at the moment for it was an unusual feeling he had at the time, passing one of the medallions to Faith.

"What should we do?" She asked him as she put the medallion down on the table.

"Well let's do what the note suggested and put them on. If there is one thing I've learned over the past few years is to trust a person who knows more than we do about things we have to face."

"But that is silly, it's like me going up to a witch who says to drink her potion because it well make me young and beautiful. Do you really think that these medallions can protect us from harm?"

"Well for one thing you don't need a potion to make you beautiful, you already are beautiful." Faith blushed when he said it. "But this is different when a mysterious person comes and leaves the medallions and a note, which says he or she knows a lot more than we do." Both of them jumped at the sound of the phone ringing.

"Hello Faith here,"

"Hi, this is Mason I just wanted to say thanks for the necklace."

"Mason I didn't leave a necklace." she looked at Alan who asked for the phone.

"Mason, hi this is Alan Tate, can you describe the piece?" Alan nodded as Mason gave him the description of the medallion. "Well both Faith and I also received one just like it. Was there a note in the box?"

"Yes, it says to wear it, for it was a special gift."

"Then do that and do not take it off, always keep it on okay."

"Okay, I'll talk to you tomorrow." she hung up. He placed the phone on the hook again.

"We should do the something." They put the medallions on and after awhile Alan went home leaving Faith alone. Taking the box into her room she put it in a drawer of her end table. Getting up and ready for bed Faith did not realize that someone was watching her. Going into the bathroom she began running water for her bathtub. Didn't realize someone was trying to get in. Coming back into the bedroom after she had finished her bath, Faith went to the closet to get her robe putting it on over her night gown as she went over to the dresser and sat down in front of the mirror to begin her nightly ritual of brushing her hair. As she was well into it she opened the top drawer to retrieve some rubber bands for her hair, looking into the mirror again and seeing a shadow on the balcony. She quickly finishes putting her hair in a ponytail. Getting up from the dresser and went the end on the opposite side of the bed, getting the peppermint spray. Strolling to the balcony doors and opened them and went out to have a look around to see if anyone was near by. Finding no one she turns back into the apartment cursing her self for being too paranoid. Closing the doors and locking them turning the off for the rest of the nigh.

Out of the shadows of the night Robert Loudon came out of his hiding place which was under the balcony ledge. Crossing the street from his car getting in he sat there and waiting for awhile, looking up to the balcony with hatred in his eyes and saying out loud to himself. (After I find those to brats you Faith McCray you will be my next victim.) Loudon let out a laugh as he started the car and drove away from the apartment. Robert Loudon enjoys what he does; he does not care about how his victims have died. If you were to look at him you think he was responding with human emotions, but if you were to get inside his mind you would find out how vile and perverted he really is and how inhuman his thoughts are for he thrives on blood. Driving down the street he made a turn in the direction of the Sheriffs' station.

CHAPTER THREE

Two weeks have passed since Kevin came into Tommy's life. Who is following him everywhere he went and that it's getting irritating, for Tommy is still not used to having another kid around because of the experience he had during school that year. He had a good time with the Bensons who were wonderful people but he did not want to leave Mason for she is the only one he wanted to have to take care of him. Sitting in his room reading a book so to get rid of Kevin for a while putting down the book he took the medallion out of his shirt to look at it again like he has done so many times before; since he had found it in the rubble that day. There was a light knock on the door.

"Enter." He quickly put the medallion back under his shirt. The door opened slowly and Kevin peeked inside to see if Tommy had something in his hand. He looked up to see Kevin peek inside. "It's okay you can come in; I'm not going to throw anything at you." Giving him a reassuring smile and then the door came wide open and Kevin entered close the door behind him. "Bored uh?" he nodded to inform Tommy that he was. Kevin drew closer to the bed where he was, and Tommy noticed for the first time that there was a necklace around Kevin's neck. Immediately see the medallion which was almost like his and he became afraid scrambling off the bed to the other side of the room to keep his distance away from Kevin.

"Who are you?" he demanded answer as his heart thumbed in his chest. Kevin was taken aback by this and did not understand the comment. Giving him a questioning looks showing Tommy that he really did not know what he was talking about. In the corner of the room he pointed to the medallion that is around Kevin's neck and then he took off his and tossed it on the bed so Kevin could see it. He picked it up and immediately he was over joy and got his knee and bowing his head in homage to Tommy. No longer afraid he stepped out of the corner and slowly went to Kevin, still on his knee he picked him up and saw tears in Kevin's eyes. Kevin wrapped his arms around Tommy and began to cry.

Tommy was taken aback by this and puts his arms around him as well. After a while Mason called from downstairs to Him. Letting go of Kevin he went to see what she wanted and walked to the top of the stairs.

"I need to stop by that bank and to run some errands could you watch Kevin while I am gone, and don't throw anything at him again, okay?" Looking up she waited for an answer.

"Sure, I'll look after him." Having many questions on his mind to ask Kevin when he got back to the room. Hearing the door close Mason had left the house. Going back to the room Kevin was waiting for him taking the medallion back from Kevin he put in back around his neck.

"Kevin, who are you?" He asks with anticipation in his voice. Holding up a finger Kevin touched his medallion and a blue haze enveloped him for a few seconds and was gone. There where Kevin stood was now a man in his place. "Where is Kevin?" Tommy said with concern in his voice.

"You wanted to know who I was so I am showing you." The man was very well muscular and wore a red uniform with a band around his forehead displaying the same symbol that was on Kevin's medallion.

"Then if you are Kevin, What is your real name?"

"I do not have a name, but I am called the Guardian." He said in a deep voice.

"So you are a protector, to whom are you suppose to protect and why?" The man smiled.

"You ask a lot of questions that is good. So let me began by telling you everything you need to know from the very start." Tommy was no longer scared of the man that stood before him and went to the bed and sat on it, for it was going to be along while that he knew just by looking at the man. "Elura is a planet that is twenty-seven light years from Earth it cannot be seen through a telescope from the Earth. There was a time when Elura was at peace and in harmony with other planets in the system for eons peace and love became a way of life for us, that is until twelve earth years ago there came the Piratains who wanted to do some tech trading with us so we allowed them to dock down on the planet's surface to talk about what kind of technology they wanted to trade. Soon as they landed they began a war with the people, since Elura didn't have any weapons they were an easy target the Piratain Emperor knew this and began to enslave its people to do the Emperor's evil deeds. The Emperor and Empress were put in hiding so they could not be found. While the war continued on the Empress had a baby boy and it was at that time the Council decided that the royal family were no longer safe on their own planet and were to be moved to a much safer atmosphere where the child could grow up away from the war. But before they were to leave it was tradition for the child to choose who will be his guardian for the rest of his life." The man smiled. "Just recently three beacons disappeared from our monitors and only one returned. The computer told us the emperor and empress were dead and that the remaining hope for Elura was still alive and in danger as time passed the council said that hope was diminishing for the Piratains found out that the boy was still alive and was looking for him, so I was sent to guard him and to teach him how to use his abilities. That boy was called the star child that was prophesied by the prophets of Elura that the star child was born with great powers and that he will restore peace and harmony to Elura and will reign for many years to come. Right now all hope of Elura is on him to remain alive." The man looks down at Tommy beholding him for the sorrow in which he felt was now replaced with joy. "You Tommy are the star child that I was speaking about the Emperor of Elura you are a very special person you have ever begun to imagine. I am so honored you chose me to be your guardian." He brings his hand up the softly brush the side of his cheek.

"When you spoke of me choosing you as a guardian in Elura dose that also mean as a parent too?" Tommy looked up not knowing how to grasp what was being said to him. He knew that he was indeed different from the other kids, but never thought that he could be that important to a world he never knew or saw.

"Yes, I am your parent, your protector, and your teacher as well as your friend." He smiled, "But I will never hurt you in any way or yell at you. You are my Emperor." Tommy was fiddling with his medallion.

"So is this the source of my powers?"

"No, not all your powers come from the medallion; most of them come from inside of you." He drew his hand away from his face.

"This is a lot to take in right now." Frowning as he stared at the medallion. "There is only one thing I miss in this world and that is my parents." Looking up as tears welled up in his eyes, getting up he put his arms around Kevin and cried out all his frustrations and anger towards the Piratains for killing his parents in cold blood and he would kill every single one of them.

"Tommy, it is not with your anger and hate you have for the Piratains that will defeat them, but it is your love and compassion you have for life. That is where your powers will be. You need to let go of all your bad feelings and began to love by doing that you are spreading peace and harmony to everyone around you. It's the best weapon you have against the Piratains. For they thrive on one thing and that is to do evil, that is what is making them stronger. You begin to do things that I have said your powers will soon be made known to you and then you will see your purpose in life more clearly, so let go of all of it even the past this is a new beginning for you and it will not be an easy one I assure you, but I will always be here for you." The phone started ringing. Kevin turned to the window. "We will start your training tomorrow."

"Okay." He ran out of the room to get to the phone picking it up on the third ring. "Hello, this is Tommy." He said while catching his breath.

"Hey kiddo, it is Mason, I was just calling to see if everything are okay with you and Kevin. Also I'm not going to be home for a while so why don't you two go ahead and fix yourselves something to eat for dinner okay."

"Alright with excitement in his voice he wanted to tell her what was going on; about the mystery of what he and Kevin are from and then he suddenly stopped himself for some reason that he did not understand but he scents that he shouldn't at least not at this time.

"After you hang up don't answer the phone just let the machine pick up the calls, and don't answer the door even if it is someone that you know understood."

"Yes ma'am I do." He hung up the phone and went back to his room.

Mason hung up the receiver on the pay phone in the lobby of Tri International Bank, going back into the bank to talk to a teller about the amount of money that is in her account. She knew the money was not hers. She walks up to a teller making sure that there was no one in line.

"Hi, how may I help you." said the male teller who wore a name tag which said Mark.

"Well I have made a transaction on the automatic teller outside and there seems to be a mistake in my balance, it shows that I have two hundred thousand and my check book balance is eight hundred. I thought that maybe it was a computer error or something."

"May I see the receipt with your account number on it?" searching her purse.

"Sure here it is." She handed it to him. Taking the receipt from Mason he then turned to his computer and entered the account number.

"Well there does not seem to be any discrepancies of any kind within the computer." Turning back to Mason who was thinking hard to remember if she by accident put in the wrong figure in on her checkbook, and couldn't recall any mistakes, for she has always been careful about that.

"Is there a date when I had made my last deposit into the account?" Taking out her checkbook to see what date she had.

"The last date was the eighteenth of June for the sum of twenty-three hundred."

"Okay then how did I wound up with two hundred thousand dollars, which is the question I have been asking you?" The teller gave her a dirty look.

"Obviously Miss Mason you didn't put your old balance in correctly, that is where the mistake is." Mason became angry with him for putting her on the spot especially in front of other people.

"Well obviously you people made the mistake and don't want your boss to find out about it; cause you don't want to lose your jobs!" she said loudly. The teller became upset and shifted from one foot to the other.

"Would you like me to get my supervisor for you?" he said in a low polite tone. Looking at his hands he seems to be having a bed day. Mason felt guilty for putting him all through this.

"No thanks, I apologize for what I said earlier and I probably made the mistake without knowing it." She smiled at him.

"It's quite alright?" He smiled a thankful smile for making his day to go a little bit easier. She grabbed her purse off the counter and she left. Outside the bank she went up the street to the real estate office. Which was a half a block walk, she finally accepted the fact that the money was hers and she attends to put it to good use.

Robert Loudon was waiting for Mason to come out of the bank. Reading the day's paper he kept watch as she came out of the bank and then proceeded to walk up the street. Starting the engine he put the car into gear and started slowly towards her, hoping that she would not catch on that she was being followed. Stopping the car as she went into another building, the car in back of him beeped its horn that he had to move so that the other drivers can pass him. Going up to the stop light he made a U-turn and parked on the other side of the street from the building and waited. Robert pulled something from the inside of his jacket and started talking into it. After the conversation he got out of the car and went to sit at a table outside the coffee house. He ordered a cup of coffee; he continued to watch the building on the other side. When the waitress came to bringing him his order, Robert recognized her from a date he once had with her. Striking up a conversation with her about how things have been at the station and in his personal life, making it known that he was still interested in her. As they were into their small talk Mason came out of the building smiling, she walked back down the street and disappeared into the crowd in the sidewalk. Robert was deep into the conversation that he did not know that Mason has left the building nor did he see her walking down the street. He continued to wait for her.

Mason unlocked her car getting in it she started it and drove off. Not really thinking where she was going and soon found herself in the child welfare department. She approached the receptionist desk asking to see Louise Bishop. The woman got up and led her into an office and asking Mason if she would like some coffee while she waited, for Louise to come back from screening a couple for adoption proceeding. Accepting her offer the woman went to go get some and was back a few minutes later with a steaming hot cup of coffee. Giving it to Mason she then turned to the door leaving Mason to her thoughts. After awhile Louise entered the office with files in her arms.

"Mason, what are you doing here?" She asked. Coming out of her day dream she looked up and there was Louise standing in front of her. For as long as she has known her Mason has never seen her so tired over work until now. Louise has fair blonde hair in curls and a tanned face that Mason always envied, but she made up for it in her figure. Louise is just the opposite shorter than Mason and was a little filled out.

"I was just wondering what was going on in finding Tommy and Kevin a replacement home for adoption?"

"Well as far as Tommy goes the Bensons had decided against adopting at this time. They told me he was a great kid but kept making them feel uneasy. For what it is worth they said that he was paranoid he kept looking behind him as if someone was following him. When the Benson's asked him why he told them that he felt as if someone was watching him, which is why they brought him back early.

"What do they expect him to do? God knows it was not ease for him to be with strangers. I can't blame him for that." She sat up in her chair.

Louise turned and went around to the front of the desk and plopped the files on its top and took her seat.

"Right now there is nothing I can do for him, but Kevin on the other hand we have not yet found out where he is from, there is no record on file that fits Kevin's description. I spoke with deputy Loudon three days ago and still they are working on it. If they do not come up with anything then he will be put up for adoption to." Leaning forward Louise put her arms on the desk looking at her friend.

"So, are we are back to square one? It's like someone does not want Tommy adopted and this big mystery about Kevin, I'm beginning to wonder." She sigh and got up getting ready to leave when Louise notice the medallion.

"Wait a minute." She suddenly said as she got up from behind the desk to stand in front of Mason. "Where did you get this?" She held the medallion piece while it was still around Mason's neck.

"Don't know it was on my doorstep two weeks ago. Why do you ask?"

"Well I saw Tommy wearing one of these." Dismissing her thought and shrugged her shoulders letting go of the medallion. She walks Mason to the office door. "You know I think I need a vacation, everyone here says that I'm working too hard, so maybe I will do just that." Running her fingers through her curly hair she turned back towards her desk. Mason did not want to get off the subject of the medallion.

"You said that Tommy has one of these?" She lifted the medallion to remind Louise of her statement.

"Yes why, are you concerned about it?"

"Well, because Kevin also has one and I don't know where they came from, I have been all over town to the jewelry stores and no one has ever seen anything like it."

"So, maybe they are a one of a kind jewelry. Mason thought and gave up on thinking too much about it.

"Maybe you are right Louise, but I just can't see it that way. I wonder if they are from overseas." Mason made a mental note to check into imported jewelry exchange. She had other things to do before she went home. Mason told Louise that she would call her later to find out about any changes in Tommy's and Kevin's situation in getting them into really good homes. She thought about the medallions and how it seemed odd for only four people that she knew have one and the fact they all appeared to be given to them by a mysterious person. The answer she wants to know is why only just them? Waving to the receptionist and told her thanks, Mason left to do the last of her errands before going home.

Sitting at the table both Tommy and Kevin ate the last of their sandwiches. Tommy got up and cleaned up the kitchen before Mason got home. Thinking about what Kevin had said about not telling her at the moment it will be a lot safer for her. Kevin also told him that he had given her and two others a medallion each telling them that since they are beginning to know too much and that would put them in danger. The Piratains will stop at nothing to get to them. Having transformed back into a boy again, was watching Tommy clean. He turned to Kevin.

"You do realize that it is just not these three who would be in danger don't you?"

"What are you saying Tommy?" Kevin spoke in a manly voice.

"Well based on what you have told me is that these Piratains are ruthless, don't you think that they may try and take over Earth next." For now he has to grow up fast for the sake of not only Elura but for Earth as well.

"Well as for right now their only goal is to find us and maybe kill us in front of all Elura just to show them that all hope is lost for them and to except the fact that their lives will changes forever and that the Piratain Emperor is then their ruler. After that they will take over Earth because of it natural resources."

"So what you are saying is that we must remain alive and to do what is necessary to kill them before that kill us right." Tommy said.

"No!" he shouted as his deep voice ranged throughout the kitchen as Tommy jumped back a little. "We do not kill, for it is not the way of peace and harmony." He softened the pitch of his voice. Looking down Tommy was taken aback by his words.

"Then tell me just how we are going to survive these maniacs. What other possible way are we going to defend ourselves if it is forbidden to kill?"

"With love peace and harmony." Kevin smiled

"Yeah right, we're putting ourselves on the firing squad line. It's suicide." He wiped the last dish dry and put it in the cupboard and turned back to Kevin. "Anyway we are not on Elura Kevin, we're on Earth and they fight back when their lives are being threatened, so why can we do the same?" Throwing the dish towel on the counter as his anger began to surface.

"We can't kill Tommy whether we are here or on Elura. It is not our way to fight back it's-" Tommy cut him off.

"I know, I know, with love, peace, and harmony, but I still think it is suicide. We can't just hide for the rest of our lives Kevin we have to make a stand some time before they find us."

"We will, but this is not the time to do that. We have to be prepared first. That is why we will begin your training tomorrow. Fighting fire with fire become a war which on one wins, but fighting anger and hostility with love and peace then the enemy will think twice about what they are doing and then try to compromise to avoid a war they will not win. Give it time, because deep down inside of you Tommy is the power you will use to win this war. Only you can use. There is none on Elura that have it, if there was Elura would have been saved a long time ago." Kevin got up from the table and went to his room leaving Tommy to think about what was just said and to allow it to sink in. Tommy was standing in the kitchen deep in thought he heard the front door open.

"Hello!" Mason yelled. "Could someone give me a hand here please?" Tommy walks into the entry hallway and saw Mason's hands were full of groceries.

"I'll take some off your hands." He grabbed two of the bags from her and went back into the kitchen.

"Where is Kevin?"

"Huh, oh he's up in his room." He sat the bags down on the table. Going back to the entry hallway he retrieved the last bag that was sitting there on the floor. Tommy returns to the kitchen and put the bag on the counter and started helping her put the items away so to make less work for her to do later. "How come you took so long.?"

"Just had a little problem at the bank that it all." Feeling tired Mason sat in a chair at the table and sighed. Running her fingers threw hair long hair. Did anyone call?"

"Nope, you were the only one." He said finishing up with the groceries he excused himself and left the kitchen.

Mason heard Tommy on the stairs and finally hearing his door close. Sitting there she thought what Louise had said about the medallion, getting up Mason want to see, but quickly decided against it. Going upstairs she went to her room to retrieve her daily planner where she had all the numbers of her friends. Soon she was on the phone with Faith McCray telling her what she had learned from Tommy's social worker, she told Faith to get a hold of Deputy Tate for Mason wanted them both at the house that evening. She then hung up; not realizing that both Kevin and Tommy were listening in on her conversation with Faith.

They went into Tommy's room where they can talk without being overheard.

"So what are we going to do now that she knows that something is going on?" Tommy said as he closed the door.

"We do nothing." Kevin started pacing the floor thinking hard.

"Do nothing; you are going to tell them about us. What happens if they turn us into the F.B.I or worse NASA?" Now Tommy started pacing back and forth. "Great now we are in big trouble."

"Tommy they wouldn't turn us in, because that would be slaughter not only for us but for them as well. We'll have to wait to see what transpires from the talk, anyway it is better for them to know what they are getting into I can understand that." Kevin smiled at him. "Be cool and relax let's play a game I am interested in the way the humans prepare the children for the world." Tommy shrugged his shoulders and got out the monopoly out of the closet and sat on the floor with Kevin sitting across from him. Both of them are waiting for the other adults to get there hoping that everything would be okay.

CHAPTER FOUR

Alan Tate was at home going through some of the reports he's taken from Loudon's desk and making copies of them putting them back so Loudon wouldn't realize they were missing. For the past two weeks he's done this and not a shred of it could be used against him except that he has been taking them before they were to be filed into the computer. Tate was thinking that maybe Loudon has a file on the computer but so far he hasn't had a chance to check into the possibility. All he can do at the time is check and recheck the reports to see if he missed anything. Looking at his notes of suspicion to mark in the computer filing and to find out where Loudon lived for as long as he known him he never thought that he may need to do some breaking and entering a home. Alan is getting desperate for answers, getting up from the table he went into the kitchen to get a beer out of the fridge. The phone ranged as he got the beer and then turned to answer it on the second ring.

"Hello," Tearing the tab off the can and taking a swig of it.

"Alan its Faith, I just got a phone call from Mason and she needs to see both of us to night. She said that Tommy has a medallion, for he didn't have one two weeks ago."

"Doesn't she know where he got it?" He said as he put the beer down on the coffee table.

"No, she didn't ask him yet, but still don't you think that it is a little weird that Tommy had a medallion after all this time?"

"No not at all, what I do think is weird is why Mason wants us over there."

"Maybe there is some thing else other than Tommy having a medallion." Faith let out a sigh for she knows that everywhere she went to find out where Kevin became from she came up empty handed and is ready to give up the search.

"Still can't find out about Kevin, huh?"

"No, I keep getting short ends, absolutely nothing."

"Well don't give up; there are still other places that I haven't had the chance to look in to. I'll bring them with me."

"Okay, you know I forgot to tell you but lately I have been followed and some one was trying to get in to my apartment at night when I'm home." Scared to be in the house alone, hoping that Alan couldn't notice her shaky in her voice.

"Why didn't you tell me before?"

"Because at first I thought that is was one of the kids at the school I teach. Now it is like this every night and I can't get any sleep, I have called the station and deputy Loudon said that he will look into the problem so far nothing is being done about it."

"Well I can see what I do about the problem okay." Alan had been seeing Faith quite a bit and found that he really liked her company for she was funny and always had something to talk about.

"Well then I will see you at Mason's; see you." Faith hung up the phone.

Alan stood there with his end still in his hand then hung it up after a minute going back to the table of copies. Looking at the clock to see that is was six o'clock one hour after the conversation with Faith. Getting up from the table going into the kitchen to get the keys leaving the light on so it would appear like there was someone else there checking everything he left by the back door to the garage.

Faith entered her apartment with her clothes that she usually have dry cleaned, draping them over the couch she went back to the door to pick up the mail off the floor and closed the door. She left the school after the call she had made to Alan telling and reminding him to meet her at Mason's, taking her things into the bedroom and putting the clothing into the closet turning back around towards the bed she saw that a white rose was put on her comforter, stunned she dropped the mail on the floor and went back into the living room she grabbed her purse and left the apartment in a hurry not bothering to close or lock the door behind her. Looking around to see if their was anyone watching her as she took her keys from her purse pressing that automatic control lock on her keychain opening the door and got in quickly locking the car door. Starting the car she sped of towards Mason's house. With her hands shaking she constantly looked in the rear view mirror to see if she was also being followed and she didn't realize how fast she was going didn't see the red stop light until it was too late. Hearing the car screeching she ran ahead on into another car.

"No!" She went through the windshield hitting the other car's windshield. Seeing everything started to spin in her head she felt really cold all over then the blackness came.

At that moment Kevin and Tommy were still playing Monopoly when a sheer pain hit Kevin looking up from the board he told Tommy that one of the three are hurt badly. "We have to see who is here." They got up from the floor and ran down stairs.

"Hey you kids," Alan said as the entered the living room.

"Where is Mrs. McCray, Mason?" Not bothering to say hi back.

"Tommy, where are your manners? We've have a guest here?" Mason was upset for them to come in without their manners attached

"We don't have time for this. Mrs. McCray is hurt badly and we got to go to her now!" He yelled which stunned Mason and Alan.

Mason got up with anger on her face. "March up to your room Tommy now!" pointing to the stair case.

"Hello isn't anybody listening to me. I said Mrs. McCray is hart badly we need to get to her before the others do." Mason stepped in front of him about ready to slap him in the face. Kevin stepped in her way looking at her with his piercing blue eyes at he touched his medallion blue light came around him and disappeared in seconds and the man standing in front of Tommy.

"Who are you?" demanded Mason as she backed away from them.

"I am the one you called Kevin and I am a guardian to Tommy who is my emperor please do what he said I will tell you all you need to know later right now we need to get to Faith McCray before the Piratains do." Kevin stood his ground when Alan pulled out his gun, about to shoot him and immediately feeling the peace and assurance inside of him. He lowered the gun to his side again.

"So what are we going to do when we get there?" Feeling like a dream that is never going to end Alan placed the gun back in the hoister.

"That is unknown right now; all I know is that the Piratains are closing in on her."

"Well then lets not waste anymore time and get in the car." Alan started for the door.

"No!" Kevin said "The car will not be fast enough, lets go into the portal we can be there in seconds." stretching out his hand a blue mist appeared with a black hole in the middle of it. The portal gave Alan the weirdest feeling that he was looking at a large eye. They one by one went in to the portal They were suddenly on the side walk and then the car crash where people coming out of there house's to look at what is going on Alan noticed the car and the body of Faith McCray lying in mangled on top of the other car which was also hit.

"No not now; can't be not now!" He started to run when Kevin caught his arm and pulled him back on the side walk, with tears forming in his eyes he looked at Kevin, "What can we do now?" Kevin was thinking fast for it would not belong before they get there, suddenly his eyes brighten up a little. He turned towards Tommy.

"Remember when I told you about love, peace and harmony, Tommy." He nodded his head yes. "Well now is the time for that, all you have to do is to think of the of them that helps the most, for what I want you to do is to freeze time all around us and hurry." putting a hand on the boy's shoulder, Tommy looks down for a moment then back up to Kevin.

"Okay I can try is all I can say right now." Closing his eyes Tommy started to think about the happy days with his family and the love he has waiting there for them. Tingling began to fill his being and then came the warmth from his hands as he extended them out away from his body slowly upwards. The others stood there and watched as streams of light came out of both of Tommy's hands meeting together above his hands, clashing without any sound became a brilliant white light radiating throughout the area, soon there was silence, and not a whisper could be heard from the neighbors who came out to see what was happening. Even the distant sound of a siren was no longer heard.

"Tommy, open your eyes." Slowly opening them not sure what to expect, seeing that everything was still and only the four of them were moving. He looked at Kevin in wonder and then in awe.

"Did I do this?" He looked around again.

"Yep, you sure did." Kevin puts his hand on his shoulder. "Now let's see what we can do for Faith." Leaving Tommy's side he went over to where Faith was laying, "She's still alive but barely." He said as Tommy approached the place where Faith laid. Mason and Allen were right behind Tommy.

"My God why is this happening? No!" Mason said, and turned her head away hoping not to vomit fighting the bale in her stomach. Alan took a hold of Mason and turns her away from the scene while trying to calm her down. Tommy drew closer to Faith, looking into her eyes which were pleading him to help her, taking one of her hands and placing it in his own he closed his eyes as he did before and thought about the good times he's had with his parents, while Kevin was thinking to fast to handle the situation and Alan, Mason still looked away as the blue glow was forming around both Tommy and Faith, the sound of bones popping and muscles snapping back into place. After a few minutes her outward appearance began to change as cuts and bruises were disappearing from her face. Tommy heard her breath normally and felt her heart beat grow stronger, opening his eyes he smiled down at her.

"How are you feeling now?" Hoping for a response from her, as she blinked her eyes a couple of times.

"Feel like new to tell you the truth doc." Smiling as she got in a upward position then was helped off of the hood of the car as Tommy continued to hold on to her hand as she began to stand on her own again. "Why is everyone looking like there about to attend a funeral referring to the others?" Mason turned back to Faith again and was astonished by what she saw Faith standing without a scratch on her.

"Could someone tell me what's going on here, she was almost dead and now she's walking and talking like nothing has happened at all." Mason said as her face turned white and then back to her natural state of color. Kevin looked up putting a hand on his head for it hurt him for bringing it up to fast, seeing Faith then looking at Tommy he immediately smiled.

"Tommy you did it." Kevin walked to where he was standing and puts his arms around him. "So now you know how to use your powers which is to listen to your heart, it will guide you through the difficult times ahead." Tommy looked up at Kevin.

"You know after all this time I thought I had lost my parents forever but they've been here all this time." Feeling good about him self now more than ever. His memory of them is now like it was yesterday, coming easier for him to remember down to the smallest detail.

Mason went over to Faith and gave her a hug, and then she went to Tommy bending down to his level,

"You know up until now I had always thought you were special and that one day you would make a difference in this world, but I had no idea you are from another, sorry for not believing in you earlier." She gave him a hug.

"That's okay; if I were in your shoes I might have done the same thing." Letting go of her he turned to Kevin. "So what do we do now?" Kevin began to tell him the things that needed done so not to leave any trail of any kind for the Piratains to discover of there being at the scene. Kevin watched Tommy work with his powers he began to see how well he was becoming adapted into using them for the good and not for evil. Also knowingly that if the Piratains get's there hands on him and knowing what he can do. They will use his powers to do their bidding. Tommy finished covering their tracks so that the Piratains would not know they were there at the scene. Then he turned to Faith's car which was crushed pretty bad and began to concentrate on it. The metal of the car started to screech loudly as it popped back into shape again and the dents of the car had disappeared...

"There I'm finished." He said. Faith went around to the driver side of the car and got in behind the wheel, starting the car she was surprised that it was running better than before. She got out of the car she wondered how a boy at Tommy's age could do things that no adult can do except working with the knowledge that they have obtained through school or gaining it through the family heritage, yet Tommy can do anything just by thinking about them.

"So, who's the big guy over there?" She pointed him out to Tommy.

"Oh, I thought you already knew. That's Kevin, you brought him over the house the night you almost hit him." She looked at him.

"You're kidding me right." She was smiling as if getting ready to laugh out loud. But looking into his face she knew that he was telling her the truth. "But that can't be him he was just a boy but much younger than you."

"I know, that's what I thought too when he transformed right in front of me." Tommy saw that she has a lot of questions that needed to be answered and that it was not the time or the place to do that. "Look I know you have a lot of questions but right now are not the time to give you those answers." He turned away from her to complete his task. Faith continued to watch him as the car disappeared from sight. After he was done, he gave her a smile and told her where the car would be which was now waiting in Mason's driveway. Kevin came over to where they were standing,

"Tommy you have to release time now. Do you think you can do that again?" Kevin was worried that he might not be able to, not knowing what the extent of using his powers for the first time.

"Sure, I think so." Feeling as if all the energy was being drain out as he uses the power he has to stop time it self, flinging his hands up like he did before, closing his eyes and he allowed the power to flow through his body. The light above his head came in a big ball which looked like it was about ready to burst from his hands, instead became smaller and then disbursed in a strange blue haze. Hearing the whispers the neighbors once again, the distant sound of the siren which was coming closer. He felt better in the time frame than he did while being pulled out of it.

Kevin quickly told the others to follow him as he went between two apartment buildings. The others were wondering what was to happen next now that they were back on the clock again, Kevin looked at the two entrances way to the alley he quickly told them to join hands and to close their eyes. They soon disappeared in the alley but inside of Mason's living room. Now that they were out of danger of being caught all of them began to relax no one said nothing for a while. Mason and Faith went into the kitchen to fix them all something to eat for the excitement of the day had built up their appetites. Faith then suddenly remembered what had happened, dropping a dish as the memory slammed into her mind as if watching a movie. The dish hit the floor she was suddenly no longer hungry. Grabbing a hold of the kitchen table feeling weak all over, Mason saw what was happening quickly went to her aide grabbing Faith gently and guiding her into a chair as Faith started shaking.

"You okay." Mason said looking concerned.

"I just remembered what happened before the crash." Her voice was shaky as she tried to regain control of her fears. Mason went to the sink and got her a glass of water. Handing the glass to her and bent down to pick up the pieces of the plate and then swept up the rest with the broom and dustpan putting the broken dish into the trash can.

"So what do you remember before," Looking down at her hands as she washed them? "You mean the accident." Knowing that if Tommy was not there Faith would have died.

""Well I was just getting home from doing some errands and when I went into my bedroom their was a white rose on the bed, at first I thought Alan had put it there but then I remembered that I had locked the door this morning and put the security alarm on before leaving for the school for my first class of the day. When I came back there was no forced entry to be found so I did what anyone else would have done, I got the hell out of the apartment not bothering or check and see if I locked up the place. I was scared like I've never been before in all my life." Faith was still shaking as she brought the glass of water to her mouth.

"Well I think Alan should know about it, maybe there is something he can do?" Mason said as she sat in the chair next to Faith giving her some moral support.

"Yea right like I can always go to Alan when ever I feel like my life is being threatened, it just would not be right especially when we are having a relationship; it would not be fair to him."

"So you two are having a relationship, that's good but if I were you I would tell him. For we almost lost you if it had not been for Tommy and Kevin." She hoped that it would sink, in her to count herself very lucky to be alive.

"You're right, I'll tell him now." Getting up from the table she and Mason took the snacks into the living room where the others were waiting for them, sitting the food down both of them sat down on the couch while Kevin and Tommy sat on the floor and Alan took the easy chair.

Kevin scented that it was time to tell them all that he told Tommy about the war on their home world and who Tommy really was how be become the hope for all Elura and about the Piratains coming to Earth to find both of them. After he had finished his story he sat down.

"This is really too much to handle, but the question is why us?" Alan said thinking that he really didn't want to get involved in a war that is taking place on another planet. He moves to pour a cup of coffee.

"Well the reason is because since you were close to finding the answers to what you wanted to know. It would be too dangerous for you if you found out too late. That is why I've gave each of you a medallion so I can know what's happening to you if you were in trouble of any kind."

Mason looked down at the coffee cup she had picked up from one of the end table. Lifting the cup from the saucer to her lips and took a sip of the sweet aroma which tasted bitter in her mouth for she had put to much sugar into it, She spoke after setting the cup back on the table. "Why not try to get the government into this, I mean if the Piratains are here than maybe they can do something about it without knowing the whole story of why they are here."

"NO!" Kevin yelled which startled everyone in the room. "I'm sorry but it will not work, once your government knows there will be more coming here and then there will be enough of them to conquer Earth and then there will be nothing lift on the planet. The smaller the number the better things will be. Any way their only concern right now is finding Tommy and me. That's all they want also they will destroy anyone who crosses their path in order to find us. I assure you, you can not be harmed as long as you are wearing the medallions, and they are what you would call a luck charm. All you have to is to set your though on the medallion and it will help you out of the situation you are in. so, I want to know if you are still willing to help us." Looking at them not wanting to invade their thoughts for he knows that they will make the right choice for their lives.

"I'm in, I don't know what we should do from here, but I'll help and do what ever I can."

"I feel the same way." said Faith

"So am I, I feel like kicking some alien butts anyway." Mason smiled as the others were laughing at her remark.

"Great, but I shall say this, it will get dangerous for the Piratains can't feel remorse and they get to the point where they feel you no longer good to them or when they pretend to like you, they will kill you. No matter how important you are to this world." Faith looked at Kevin with concern in her eyes.

"Do they become infatuated with someone and then kill them." she asked Kevin, Mason knew where the question came from.

"Yes they do, why do you ask?"

"The reason I asked was because I think I am being stalked by one of them." She retold them what had happened before her unfortunate accident.

"Has there been any one besides me whose been coming to your apartment lately?" Alan said while thinking with concern weather or not Faith should return to her apartment by her self.

"Yes only Deputy Loudon, no one else that I know of." Alan sat up quickly when he heard Loudon's name being mentioned, then he settled back into the easy chair.

"Kevin, is there anyway we can tell if there Piratain or not?"

"Well, in a way there is one. On their face they will have a scar that runs from the ear to the chin. That is the only way that I used to identify them."

"Are they peopling like us?" Faith said now feeling better now that the mystery of who Kevin is and where he came from.

"No." Kevin shook his head. "As a matter of fact they are the ugliest creatures you ever want to see. The bodies they are in are human which makes them a host inside so not to reveal their true nature. They would kill the person first and then join theirs with the one they just killed. That's when the scar appears just after they enter the body."

"Yuck, like the movie I had recently seen."

"You mean there has been some of his kind here before?" Kevin asked with wonderment on his face.

"No, what I just said was a show that I watched on the T.V." Mason pointed to the big screen that sat in the corner of the living room.

Alan looked at his watch and realized that he had to be going for he had to be at the station in an hour. He got up from the chair about ready to leave.

"Faith, are you going to go back to your apartment tonight?"

"Yes, just to go pick up some things and return here, that's if it's okay with Mason if I stay here for a couple of days." She looked at Mason for an answer.

"Sure that will be just fine." Faith also stood up to leave to get some things from her apartment.

"Great I'll follow you in my car, and leave the apartment when you do." Alan hugged her.

"That's fine with me." She returns his squeeze. Mason had walked with them to the door and told Faith that she will see her when she got back, then she closed the front door. Turning around Kevin was back into being a boy again, shaking her head she thought;(I better start getting use to his changing like that.) Kevin smiled as he read her thoughts.

CHAPTER FIVE

Loudon sat in an unmarked car watching Faith pull into the driveway. Leaving the motor running she went inside the apartment. After a couple of minutes went by, Faith came back outside with a suit case in her hand turning around to make sure the door was locked and the alarm system is working. Loudon continued to watch her he suddenly saw Alan Tate walking up the driveway to the running car. Opening the car door for her Faith got behind the wheel and Alan then closed the car door then went to the front door making sure it saw secured. Loudon saw Faith sticking her head out the window calling out for Alan. He thought. At the sight of Tate Loudon's hands gripped around the steering wheel while seeing Tate bending down towards Faith's face and kissed her. When Alan came up, Loudon looked at him with hate in his eyes, (Every time she's there you are too Deputy Tate, but I will fix that, so you will not see her again.) Loudon thought to himself as he chuckled at the ways his mind has been working lately, putting his car in gear as he saw Faith backing out of the driveway and Tate walks towards his car, hurrying so she could get out, for he had parked right in front of the driveway. Loudon didn't start to follow her until Tate had gone on his way. Keeping a safe distance from her, so that she wouldn't know that she's was being followed. Turning off the street Faith lived on, Loudon was deep in thought when the beeping started to sound, turning his car to the curb He looked both ways into the traffic and on the opposite side of the street making sure he wasn't being watched, reaching over to the glove compartment, opening it he took out a small crystal object in his hand then pushing some buttons where the glove compartment was supposed to be hollow instead it was a computer of some kind, for there was nothing in the world like it. Putting the crystal piece to his mouth Loudon began talking in to it. After giving a report to his superior, he waited for a reply to come.

"Loudon!" the voice yelled in English. "You were suppose to find the star child, not going around running after an earthling woman to satisfy your desires, remember that the Emperors commands are to be carried out before yours are!" said the superior in a authorized voice, "Plans have changed, instead of killing the star child, bring him to me. Then the Emperor will show all of Elura that their last hope of a savior will die right in front of their eyes and to show them once more that he means business, and if anyone gets in your way you bring them along as well. We can not afford the government to know what we are up to and who we are. As for the Elura-thing who escaped, kill him now get back to work or else you will be replaced is that clear!" The superior voice boomed out at Loudon. He knew that being replaced meant death for failure to complete his mission.

"Yes superior, I am on it." He said in a nervous voice, putting the communicator back into the glove compartment he quickly started the car putting it in gear he drove off not spending any more time thinking about Faith, only that he will deal with her later.

He had been following Mason around finding out that she was taking care of two children one of them just arrived; he knew very well that it is the Elura-thing who escaped and that other was the star child. He knew about it when Tate was filling out the report about the boy who survived the blast six months back and he had taken the report out of the box which is the one that was meant for the computer so that they can be worked on in a later date. Loudon knew he could not allow that to be put into the computer so he took it and put it in his desk where they couldn't be noticed missing also taking the accident reports that he had caused to cover his own tracks. He continued to drive as he quickly devised a plan to get them both and off guard when they lease expected him to go after them. For Loudon will take on another form one that they will trust implicitly. He drove into the child welfare department parking lot. Getting out of the car and went inside the building, seeing the receptionist not at her desk he when in to the office area and right into Louise Bishops office. Loudon saw that she saw not in and decided to wait for her to come back into the office. Looking around and then hid behind the door so he would not be notice when she entered.

Louise Bishop was on her way to see Mason, to get some information from her about Kevin, also to see if he can tell her one last time where he came from, if he couldn't tell her anything else she doesn't know then she will put him threw the adoption system which she desperately hated, because all the government really wanted was the money, it didn't care about the child unless it was forced to care forced to care by the people in the state. For now they are too busy running their own lives to care what happens. Louise didn't blame them at all because she was able to identify with them. Sometimes it does get too difficult to care about others even when it's the children who are the future of this world and maybe one day there may come such a person in to power who will not care what happens to them just because when he or she was little no one care about them., stopping at the intersection, pulling out her cell phone and dialed Mason's number.

"Hello,"

"Yes, is Mason in, this is Louise Bishop."

"Just a minute." he said

"Hello, this is Mason."

"Hi Mason darling, its Louise Bishop, I am on my way to see you I thought that I should call you so that you know. There are some things that we need to discuss about the boys." She looks through her daily planner for the right documents that needs to be filled out before the adoption could be process. Finding that she had forgotten about the papers she left on her desk at the office.

"Sure you can come." Mason said.

"Okay, great I'll be there in awhile I forgot some papers that I need for you to fill out back at the office."

"Well see you then." Mason then hung up.

She cursed her self for leaving without the papers, making a u-turn and headed back to the office. Not knowing what was a waited there for her, but the cold darkness of her death.

Loudon was still standing behind the door waiting for the final stage of the body to make its transition into Louise. Normally they would just dissolve it so that it can't be found. Loudon's body was being preserved so that it can be used again, the creature didn't want anyone knowing that Loudon was missing; completely out of the body the creature dangled on the wall like a fly would do then positioned itself right above the door hanging on the ceiling like some kind of decoration. Louise entered the office and went straight to the desk without any hesitation; suddenly the creature drops down on her snapping her neck with easy and started merging with the body while it was still warm. Few minutes later Louise came out of the office closing and locking the door behind her. The receptionist came towards her,

"Miss Bishop here is the papers that you forgot to take with you."

Louise looked at her at her like she didn't know what she was talking about the creature inside was so confused for it couldn't obtain any of Louise's memories and for a second was totally unsure of herself so she took the papers and acted like she knew what the girl was talking about then walks on without thanking her which is what the real Louise would have done.

"Mrs. Bishop, are you okay? You don't look so good." said the receptionist. Louise turned to the girl and gave her a weak smile that was saying she would be okay. "I'll be over Mason's house to talk with her so I don't know when I'll be back." Louise said over her shoulders as she walking out of the building to the parking lot. The receptionist watched her drive off in a different kind of car, shrugging her shoulders she came to the conclusion that Louise had bought another car and when on about her business.

Mason had been upstairs packing some of the kid's bags. Alan Tate said that they may not be safe any longer. He drove by after several hours and told her to pack each of them a bag of clothing according to what Kevin said to him. About this being the tip of the iceberg and that things are only going to get worse from here on out. Mason thought about what she is going to tell Louise. She knew that the truth will only alarm her even more and knowing Louise she attends to blow things out of per portion getting her agitated will only cause her to worry about the kids. Mason smiled as she remembered how she was when she wanted to take Tommy out of the city for awhile during the weekend and she pitched a fight because she couldn't come along. Setting the two bags down next to Kevin's room and was about to knock on the door when the door bell ranged down stairs. Making her jumpy because of the things that were happening although she was inspecting Louise to bring by the papers she needed to fill out on Kevin. She opened the door and welcomed Louise into the house.

"Hi" "come on in." opening the door wider so she could enter.

"So how are you doing today Mason?" Louise said.

"I'm okay I guess, just been running around the house working on some chores and the usual." She leaned against the door and forgetting her manners at the time, she was about to let Louise inside of the house when Kevin came down the stairs with Tommy right behind him. The door opened wider and Kevin looked up seeing Louise he stopped suddenly turning to Tommy as if to say they are here, immediately Tommy alarmed Mason.

"Mason," he said as he began to slowly back up the stairs allowing Kevin to do the same. "That's not Mrs. Bishop!" yelling to her to make her aware of the danger she was in. Acting on impulse Mason tried to shut the door it slammed into Louise Bishop face, hearing the door making contact with her face then the sound of flesh against the cement. She dead bolted the door as both boys helped her to draw the curtains so the Piratain will not know where they are at in the house.

Faith was in the kitchen making herself a sandwich when Mason came bursting in. startling her caused Faith to lose her sandwich to the floor,

"What's wrong as she watch Mason checking to see if the backdoor was locked and drew the curtains in the kitchen? Turning to Faith and said two words,

"No drill" she shouted Faith set to work on her part, picking up the phone to call the sheriff station and finding the phone line dead. Faith ran to the living room and grabbing her purse and pouring the contents out on the coffee table until her cordless phone fell out of the purse and thought (NEVER LEAVE HOME WITHOUT IT.) opening it she quickly dialed the stations number.

"Hello Tate speaking." Faith did not give him time to finish.

"Alan its happening get, over here quick." she then hung up not saying another word. She looks around the room for something to defend herself with and realizes they were not dealing with humans but an alien. The door in the front there was a sickening sound of wood breaking. Faith saw that it not hard for the intruder to get in. Mason came in upon hearing the door crunch like a tooth pick it was being broken, in just minutes Louise was inside the house looking at both of them, smiling she went towards them. Mason and Faith backed up about to take a chance on running into the kitchen again, smiling Mason said to Faith.

"You remember how crazy it was when you finally trap a mouse."

"Yeah," Faith answered thanking Mason silently for helping her not to get out of control.

"Guess whose running into the kitchen now." They dashed into it knocking the chairs in Louise's way to make it a little harder to catch them.

"Why not think like a mouse." She yelled diving under the table picking it up from underneath and went right into Louise knocking her down. Hearing her cry out in pain, gave her a delightful surge of pleasure knowing that she had actually hurt it. Faith then went for the silverware drawer and to the knife rack, gathering them up and started throwing them at her hoping to stall Louise from regaining her footing.

"ENOUGH!!" Louise yelled in pain and in anger for wanting revenge and was not able to do what pleased it most. The yell ranged loud in the kitchen. Faith had thrown a steak knife at Louise catching her in the shoulder. Louise looked in the direction where the knife was thrown seeing Faith Louise gave her a sickly smile; grabbed the knife from her shoulder and slowly took it out. Faith saw there was no blood coming from the wound, standing there as she felt the blood in her own body began to drain from her face.

"AHHH," Louise dropped the knife. Looking hard at her and grinning from ear to ear. "By the way I didn't get a chance to ask you. How did you like the rose I left you on the bed?" Louise laughed watching Faith crumble to the floor, "I thought it was quite nice of me to do that for you, don't I deserve a kiss from you." She came in to the room and went towards Faith who was now crouched on the floor leading against the cabinet doors with her head between her legs and her arms wrapped around her knees looking worse than before. Mason saw Louise was drawing her strength from Faith's fears and how she was fully unattended, like she wasn't even there, decided she had to do something before it was too late for Faith, scanning the kitchen with her eyes for something large, she spotted the butchers block just in front of her and the iron skillet laid on top. Mason waited for Louise to come further in to the kitchen before she could reach and act.

"Yes, I was watching you everywhere you went, until Tate started ruining my plans for us to be together, but of course you just had to kiss him instead, well I decided if I can't have you neither can he." Louise was now a few feet from her victim. Just as she was going to say more Mason came at her from behind, hitting Louise on the head hard with the skillet vibrated in her hand making her bones ache. Louise turned around with fury in her eyes. "How dare you!" she put her hand on the back of her head, "You put a dent in my head!" Mason saw Louise had hit her boiling point, seeing the rage in her eyes Mason didn't have time to react when Louise's hand shot out and grabbing her by the throat lifting her off the ground, snapping her neck, Louise threw her across the room and watching Mason's body hit the wall hard leaving an imprint as she fell to the floor. She turned back around to face Faith who was no longer crouched on the floor, but gone. Louise went out of the kitchen looking for both the kids and Faith.

Tommy and Kevin came out of there hiding spot they knew it was not going to stop unless they both surrender. They quickly came down the stairs hearing Louise screaming for Faith to come out of hiding or she will die if she was found. Tommy and Kevin entered the living room, they saw Faith up against the side of the door frame white as a ghost trembling uncontrollably holding the Medallion in her hand, not seeing the boys for her eyes were closed as she concentrated on the medallion. Kevin touched his changing into his true form turns to Tommy.

"Stay here and keep an eye out for Deputy Tate." He turns towards the kitchen, walking in he saw how much of a fight Mason and Faith had endured while they were hiding upstairs, looking around he saw Mason mangled body and wondered how he couldn't sense it. Hearing the sound of broken glass behind him Kevin quickly turned around.

"Well Elurain, it's your turn to die." Louise said as she lifted the medallion up for him to see it. "Even your magic didn't do much good." she said in distaste throwing the medallion away from her.

"She forgot how to use It." he said, "She knew what she was getting into, saving a life is considered an act of love to the person she was protecting."

"I will find her and kill her the same way I will do you" Laughing she reached for Kevin.

"Not so fast dude;" Tate said behind her as he entered the kitchen. "You have to get through me first."

Louise turned slowly around for she knew whose voice that was and wasn't going to underestimate it.

"Well Tate I see you finally made it to the last dance of the day, what took you so long to get here?" Tate was fully faced with the woman he knew from working on Tommy's case in the beginning of his parent's death.

"Alan, don't let her fool you she is not Louise Bishop, it's a Piratain in her body." Kevin said with conviction in his voice hoping to alarm him.

"I know who she is, isn't that right Loudon, I found your body in the office of the late Louise Bishop, and do you think you can disguise yourself as her knowing I have already put you on the most wanted list in this state and soon other states will have your picture on their board and on the T.V. in a matter of hours." He held up a trigger box in his hand, "Unless you let the boys go it will not happen." Louise knew she just had been caught red handed fail to recover the star child turned to Tate.

"You may think you have won but this is far from over." A bright spot as big as a golf ball came out of her stomach and spread out through her entire body; until there was nothing left of the Piratain. Kevin saw this happen too many times to know what it all meant.

"Where did she go, where did the Piratain go?" Tate said when it disappeared.

"The Piratain is what you call dead; since he did not complete his mission he killed himself for it would have been far worse death at the hands of the Piratain Emperor." Kevin said when he went to where Mason laid dead, he knew nothing can be done for her he stood there for a moment just looking at her as if trying to remember her the way she was before. He turns leaving the kitchens not wanting Tommy to come in and see her like that, Kevin wanted him to remember her the way she used to be. Alan waited until he was gone taking the table cloth off the floor covering Mason up. Jolts of memory came flooding in, like a nightmare out of control, the gun shots ranged loud in his head putting his hands to the ears to stop the sounds from coming to him. He turned away from the body and hurried out of the room not wanting to deal with it again. He took his hands away from the ears, fines that he was still shaking from the terror that is still in his mind eating away at him like a disease only he can cure. Faith saw him ran into his arms and cried, babbling something about not being able to help Mason. Faith blamed her self for Mason's death.

"She would still be alive if I hadn't choked like I did." She pulls away from him, and looked into his eyes which seeming to tell her he understood how she felt at that moment. He then turns away because he could not tell her in words; he still has not forgiven himself for what happened years ago. Faith brought her hand to his chin and raised it so that his eyes where looking into hers. He saw her face was streaked with mascara from all the crying she had done.

"It's not your fault. Mason knew what she was doing." Alan knew there was no escaping her eyes brought his lips to hers and gently kissed her. wanting to take her pain but knew his was too much to carry himself, she grabbed his hand as they past by the caved in door stepped outside with Kevin and Tommy who were huddling together Kevin told him Mason did not survived the ordeal. Alan wondered if Tommy will ever be able to rule his people on Elura, will they ever make it as far as tomorrow. He had no idea but knew they must survive not only for the Elurain people but Earth as well. What ever they need to do they better do it fast before more of them are on our tail?

"What is the next step Kevin?" He said in a dull voice looking at a boy/man who knows how these aliens work.

"We wait." he said.

"WAIT! AFTER THEY KILLED MASON AND NOW THEY ARE ANGRY EVEN MORE BECAUSE THEY DIDN'T GET WHAT THEY WANTED, AND WE SIT HERE TO BE DEAD MEAT TO WAIT!!" he yelled out of frustration couldn't believe what Kevin just said to him.

"We are waiting for a man his name is Troy Beckman of the F.B.I. Thanks to you I have to make sure that he doesn't get hurt." Kevin looked at Alan like he was looking at a kid with his hand in the cookie jar. Getting up he folded his arms, "You have not only put him in danger but could have put your world in danger of being blown to pieces the Piratains have the capability to blow up planets and believe me when I say they are forming a habit of doing it." He continues to look at him. "I said not to contact anyone of the government and what did you do? You went and done the exact opposite." Kevin threw his arms up. Tate looked at him.

"I had no choice, if I don't do it now there will be a panic all over the place, is that what you want to happen? Kevin looked to the ground

"Well of course not, that will kill a lot of your people."

"That is one of the reasons why I contacted the government so that the people can be put at ease and the other reason is because Loudon was one of those things I thought that if the government can find away to kill them then we can use that weapon against the Piratains."

"That's the kind of thing we want to avoid, Alan we can't kill, it is beyond our ability to do that. Anyway the Piratains are stronger then us, and faster." Alan shook his head.

"I don't understand, why do your people have such compassion for them and yet they want to destroy all you have accomplished, it just not right." Alan said. Leaning against on of the pillars he was frustrated. Both of them perked up their heads when the sirens came closer to them. Kevin turns around and went back inside the house and returned with Mason's medallion.

"We have to go now, there isn't much time for me to tell you everything you want to know, but we got to get moving." Kevin went over to Tommy who was still in tears mourning over the death of Mason.

"Will you be able to make a portal Tommy?" Kevin asked softly.

Nodding his head he stood up wiping his eyes on his sleeves, closing his eyes he heard the sound of crackling thunder. He opened his eyes looking back at the house he knew he will never see again.

"Tommy lets go." Kevin grabbed him and went into the portal everything disappeared behind them as the end of it had automatically closed by itself.

CHAPTER SIX

So many cars had surrounded Mason's house, police men and other people from different agencies from across the United States to find out what had happened there. According to the witness who claim to have seen four people disappear into thin air. He told the police that it sounded like a war was going on in there because that's what it sounded like. The rest of the neighbors didn't hear or seen anything at all.

Agent Troy Beckman was coming up the block when he noticed the whole street from the house on down the side of the road there were so many people busy about there jobs hoping the press doesn't get in and try to cause trouble or panic for the people. Troy rolled down his window to shows his I.D. and his badge without a word being spoken.

"Okay Agent Beckman you can go right in." pointing in the direction where he can park his car. Troy nodded his head indicating that he understood and drove on. Entering the house he holds up his badge to silence anyone who dared to speak against him. Going straight into the kitchen where the body of Mason Hollenbeck was found, picking up the table cloth that was still covering the body He notice how the body was lying as if someone or something just picked her up easily crushing her throat and throwing her into the wall which parts of her body was imprinted into the wall. Shaking his head he knew his work had been cut out for him, if only he can see what the future had in stored for him Troy Beckman would choose to run away rather than face it with all he's got.

Troy Beckman is a type of a guy that every man envies, blonde hair, blue eyes and a body that any man would kill for. Most people think "with a body like that I can do or be anything I want to be." Looking at Agent Beckman anyone would groan in agony of want for he seems to have everything a man could want, which is not entirely true with Troy, who seems to keep to himself not wanting to get close to anyone for fear that they would die on the spot. Also there were dark secrets he doesn't want anyone to know about, when he had gotten his orders from Agent Winters who suspects that something big was going on because of the information he's gotten from a deputy Tate. Troy didn't trust Tate's information because they would have been false. Making the whole trip up there be useless, but the more he dug the more he believed that in deeded something was going on. He immediately pack and over night bag and left for Fairfax, Virginia. At the moment he stood over Mason's body wondering why she had to get the short end of the stick even in death that's what she got.

Little did he know that Mason had served her purpose just as he will soon serve his?

"Hello, Agent Beckman." Said the man who knew he was sent from Washington D.C. to investigate the murder of Mason Hollenbeck and of Louise Bishop who was missing as well. Beckman looks up.

"Yes, how can I help you?" He said in a cool voice of a person who knows what he's doing.

"Hi, I'm Dr. Hendrix I was told to talk to you about Mason Hollenbeck's body, and was wondering if you want me to do an autopsy report on her to see if there is anything else we can find out who her attacker was?" He looked at down at the covered body. "What a waste of life." Dr. Hendrix said.

"I agree no I don't want a full autopsy just get some blood and tissue samples, which will be all on that." Dr. Hendrix nodded his head as he wrote down his orders then he went off to his other duties. Agent Beckman took a look around the kitchen hoping to find any thing out of the ordinary. Seeing nothing he left the kitchen and went upstairs to the bedrooms. He enters into one of the bedrooms, noticed there were bags already packed for there quick get away from what ever was stalking them and never had a chance to come back for them. He turned to one of the officers.

"Is there any pictures of the two boys?" He asked.

The officer stood up from getting the finger prints off of the door knob.

"We haven't found any yet, but we are going through our files to see if there is any resent reports on the two boys." He was interrupted by another voice.

"Sergeant, I've found something." Wearing a pair of latex gloves the officer approached the sergeant, handing him a plastic bag which contained the newspaper clipping about the incident that happened just a half a year ago. The sergeant gave the clipping to Agent Beckman.

"I remember this, only a boy named Tommy survived the explosion that happened inside of the house, but the weirdest thing is we couldn't find a thing or any possible cause to the explosion and get this the boy walked out of the flames unharmed, its the strangest thing you ever seen, also the neighbors heard nor saw anything about it. After this was printed Tommy wasn't the same kid anymore." shrugging his should to avoid the unpleasant feeling he was getting.

"Are you to telling me that kids and adults were actually afraid of him? Because he survived an explosion that was impossible for anyone to come out of it alive with out a scratch on him is that about right?" He looked at the sergeant to his reaction on his face.

"How did you know about that? It wasn't suppose to go into government until the sheriff's department finishes there investigation." seeing the man holding up the file on Tommy and on the explosion.

"Its all in here, a deputy Alan Tate put it in the computer this morning, is there anyway I can get a hold of him, there are some questions I need to ask him."

"Sure, I'll see what I can do." The sergeant walks away from Beckman pulling his walkie-talkie off the clip he spoke to the dispatcher asking her to get a hold of the sheriff's department. Finished with that he returns to Agent Beckman. "I'm still waiting for answer from the sheriff station." At that moment the walkie-talkie began to crackle to life, picking it up, the sergeant spoke quickly into it after he got the response he was waiting for. Signing off he then looked at Agent Beckman. "Sheriff Wilson is coming over here." The sergeant said nothing else and went back to what he was doing. Beckman left the room finishes his rounds and looked over the room to see if anything was missed. He was on the way down when there was shouts of angry voices coming from the living room, reaching the bottom of the stairs Agent Beckman was watching two officers try to hold on to an old man who had managed to drag two officers a few feet from where they started, finally a third officer came at him in the midsection bringing him down like a common criminal.

"I am an officer of the law, you morons so get off of me!" He yelled in frustration, one of the officers dug into the man's pocket to get his ID looking at it he showed the other officer and they both let him up slowly and apologized to him. The older mans face was beet red with eyes ready to kill, "I would like to see the person in charge here." He asked as he straightened his uniform tie.

"I am Agent Beckman and the one in charge of this operation, is there anything I can do for you." Beckman extended his hand out to the older man.

"I'm Sheriff Wilson, I wish I could say it's a pleasure to meet you, but under these circumstances." Taking the hand and shook it, while turning his head he scowled at the three officers who were still watching him.

"I take full responsibility for my men; sorry that you had to go through this I forgot to tell security that you were coming. So as you can see we're very busy." Beckman said hoping that Sheriff Wilson would get right to the point not wasting anymore of his time, not to be plain out rude to him after all Sheriff Wilson deserves the same respect that he does.

"Yes, well two of my men are also missing as well Agent Beckman. Deputies Robert Loudon and Alan Tate neither one of them has reported back to me during the last three hours and I know that they are tied up in this case somehow, the reason I have my suspicions is that Deputy Tate was working on the case after it had been closed." Agent Beckman listened to the Sheriff's story.

"Well, that could explain the two cars we've found." Beckman went to an officer who was taking notes down in his black book so he could rewrite them in his police report later on. "Officer Duncan, do you still have the notes you took down about the two car found abandoned?" Duncan nodded his head to Beckman. "Well," said Beckman.

"Oh, umm let's see." He waited for Duncan to find it, he felt like he was being watched from behind him. He turned in the same direction that he just came. Seeing the same three officers who gave Sheriff Wilson a hard time was still standing there watching every move he made?

"Get back to work!" His voice boomed, immediately they dispersed and went back to do what they were doing before. Duncan was waiting for his full attention.

"One of the cars was found in the child welfare Department, we got the trace on the license plate it was registered to Deputy Loudon, the other is a sheriff's car it is assigned to Deputy Tate and it was found here." Finishing informing the two men, he looked up at Agent Beckman waiting for anymore questions he might have him answer.

"Thanks Duncan, that is all for the time being." Duncan nodded his head and went back to his taking notes on the scene.

"One thing that puzzles me is that Loudon's car was found in the child welfare dept." said the Sheriff.

"Maybe he went to see Louise Bishop for some information for a case he was working on at the time he disappeared?" seeing the Sheriff shaking his head in protest.

"No, that would be unlikely, because Loudon never showed up for duty early this morning. Tate was at his desk on the computer putting in some reports and made some phone calls then left the station like I've never seen him run. That was around ten o'clock this morning."

Agent Beckman remembered that it was about the same time that he had gotten the call from Washington asking him to look into it.

"Sheriff Wilson, the F.B.I. had received some reports from Deputy Tate and he said in the report that two boys were in need of protection and when he tried to tell you that this you wouldn't listen to him." Looking at the sheriff who looks like a loin caught and is looking for another way out.

"So he told you guys about the incident that took place a couple of months ago?"

"Yes, he did. Why didn't you want the report filed?" Agent Beckman asked.

"Well, it was incomplete and we have not finished with investigating and trying to find the cause of the accident. That is why we didn't file it." He said knowing very well that Agent Beckman knew this.

"Then why did you start suspending Deputy Tate for doing his job?" The sheriff looked at Agent Beckman as if he had just been hit in the stomach.

"Waite a minute, first of all it was not deputy Tate's case to work on but deputy Loudon's and ever since then those two have been at each others throats. If you ask me I see Tate as a problem, sticking his nose where it didn't belong." The sheriff was getting red with anger for he didn't need a big shot coming into his town telling him how he should do his job.

"Sheriff Wilson!" He yelled, "If you would have just taken time out to listen to what deputy Tate was trying to tell I would not be stand here cleaning up a mess that could have been prevented, because of you not doing your part I have six people missing and one dead sticking your nose where it doesn't belong is every officers motto in case you've have already forgot." Beckman saw that every one had stopped what they where doing, seeing Duncan, he waved him over,

"Officer Duncan, would you please escort Sheriff Wilson off of these grounds and make sure he doesn't get back in. Also I want every file on anything you think may have a connection with the so call accidental explosion and I want you to go thru Loudon's and Tate's desk, see what you can dig up over at the station. Take some of the officers you trust only, you got that." Watching Duncan writing something's down in another pad.

"Yes sir." Taking the Sheriff by the arm and leading him out of the house shouting threats at Agent Beckman as he was lead away. Beckman went to the kitchen entrance to see one more time if he could find anything that will point him in the right direction to the others that are missing. Keeping them alive is his primary goal at the moment, looking around at the damaged kitchen-and thinking out loud who or what ever did this was very strong, Dr. Hendrix came in the kitchen he was looking for him.

"Agent Beckman, I thought you had already left. We've found some papers in one of the boy's room. I think it was found in the one that is name Tommy." The officer gave him the paper that some strange marking it is something that Beckman had never seen before.

"So, you're the expert Doc what do you think this is suppose to be?" Beckman was still looking at the piece of paper trying to remember if he had seen it before.

"Well you see here, pointing to the top of the outer circle, it looks like its some kind of a medallion." Beckman shook his head in agreement with him, "just for the record, I'm a pathologist not a gemologist. Anyone could tell you that." seeing Beckman crack a smile at his own mistake.

"Oh sorry," He said. He was hoping that he wouldn't have to explain himself to the doctor.

"No offense taken I know that you have a lot of things going on all at once, so I understand where you are coming from I often make that mistake myself, well I'm done here, I will have a pathology report ready for you by tomorrow morning." Doctor Hendrix started to leave.

"Why, did you bring me this instead of one of the officers?" He asked.

"I'm a collector of very rear jewelry and I have never seen a piece like that, it is a very unusual piece."

"How unusual is it?" Beckman began to get curious and interested about it. "Well, as you can see the markings are like a story book, you know the old saying that a picture is worth a thousand words?" Doctor Hendrix looked at Beckman in a way that if you allow him he would talk your ears off, for that is what he was most interested in.

"Thanks for the information I will look into this myself." The doctor waved at him as he left the kitchen area. Beckman found him self alone once again, standing there he thought of some possibilities of where he can start looking for answers. Hoping that this will not be the only thing they have to go on. For he can smell danger is just around the next corner. He left the house and drove over to the station. Entering the station Duncan was in the front of the office waiting for him to get there.

"Sir we've found a lot of files inside of deputy Loudon's desk, and then tried to see if they were in the computer they were not, plus we've found samples that were collected at different scenes and guess what we've found Loudon's finger prints on them and one more thing there were no other prints on the samples that were taken. So what I figure is that Loudon was trying to cover his own tracks and Tate must have found out who knows what happened next." Duncan sounded really excited about the fact they finally have a break through and a suspect as well.

"Has the prints been confirmed?" Beckman said

"Yes, sir they have been confirmed by the one person who did the print analyzing."

"Who was that?" He saw the grin on Duncan's face. Don't tell me, Sheriff Wilson was the analyzer."

"That's correct sir." Duncan said. Upset that Beckman didn't allow him the thrill of telling him what he had accomplished. But the thought was pushed from Duncan's mind. He knew it was unprofessional acting like a child in a candy store.

"Does he know what you found out?" He asked, not caring about anything else at the moment.

"Yes, he is being contained in his office right now."

"Well, done." said Beckman as he followed the officer to the Sheriff's office. "Sheriff Wilson what a surprised to have you with us so soon." The Sheriff looked at him like he didn't know what he was talking about. Agent Beckman enters taking off his suit jacket and hanging it across the chair, waking over to the window he brought the blinds down and closing them. He saw that on one was in the deputy office area Duncan had already closed it off.

"Okay, lets cut through all the bull and get right down to the heart of the matter, Why did you cover for deputy Loudon when you knew he was the one doing the killings and covering them up along with other things as well?" He looked hard at Sheriff Wilson.

"I don't know what the hell you are talking about, I've done nothing wrong. I'm not going to say anything else until I talk to a lawyer, I know my rights!" He stood up form behind his desk. Duncan had come up behind the Sheriff while Beckman was talking to him. Putting both of his hands on the Sheriff's shoulders he shoved him back into his chair. Sheriff Wilson began to get angry he knew the reason why and what Agent Beckman was going to get from him whether Sheriff Wilson likes it or not.

"Your not going to be talking to a lawyer, but the Internal Affairs for your crimes, as of this moment you have no rights so might as well start chucking it up." Beckman returned to the chair leaning on the back he observed the way that Sheriff Wilson was acting, he noticed the Sheriff was getting redder by the minute.

"You, fools I am not what I appear to be!" His voice started to change at the same time Duncan's hands began to burn on the Sheriff's shoulders, he screamed out in pain removing his hands off of his shoulders. "That should teach you to keep your hands to your self boy!" The Sheriff laughed as he stood back up from the desk. Duncan moved away from him. The Sheriff continued to watch Beckman face expressions of fear but saw none he turns to Duncan who couldn't believe what he just felt for the pain in his hands were getting better, still he was afraid and caught off guard. "Agent Beckman this mans blood is going to be on your hands." He grabbed Duncan's neck from behind him, while he was still on the floor. The thing that no longer looked human wretched the officer up so easily Duncan looked like a rag doll about to be torn apart by its angry owner. At an instant the office door came open.

"Let him go!" That startled everyone in the room, all eyes turned to see who it was, and saw Tommy standing there.

"Well, look who just joined us. The little Emperor of Elura coming to the rescue to save a pitiless life. So where are the others, are they with you?" The Piratain said. Not making a move.

""No I am here on my own free will, it is me you want so let him live." The Piratain dropped Duncan on the floor and turn towards Tommy.

"You knew we were looking for you and you knew very well that you are going to be taken back to Elura so the people can watch their only hope be muffled out." Greed became the important thing to the Piratain, was told by his superiors that the one who brings back the child Emperor will be rewarded the right hand at the Emperor's throne.

"I know what your intentions are and I have to say that you are sadly mistaken, I will not allow you to destroy what my parents worked their entire lives for Elura they gave their lives not only to save the planet, but to save me as well. Their deaths will not be in vain, but to usher in the beginning of a new era. Not only to set Elura free but of all to save Earth." Tommy saw Beckman slowly going for his gun. He shook his head from side to side allowing the Piratain to see what Beckman was about to do.

"YOU FOOL!!" Smacking him across the face Troy Beckman stumbled across the floor and quickly regaining his balance and was about ready to charge at the Piratain who suddenly grabs a hold of him by the throat. "THIS IS NOT YOUR WAR SO STAY OUT OF IT IF YOU KNOW WHATS GOOD FOR YOU!!" After staying that the Piratain lifted Troy off the floor his feet were not touching the ground and was about ready to kill him.

"I told you to stop, I can't allow you to take another human beings life. You are told to follow orders or would you prefer them to do the same thing they did to the one you called Loudon." He heard this and slowly let him down.

"How do I know you are telling me the truth?" The Piratain said, keeping his hand around Beckman's throat.

"You know as well as I do that an Elurain can never lie. I am of my word."

"Prove it then, so I may know that you are of your royal word." He smiled as he waited for Tommy to speak again. Lowering his head he began to think and knew the only way to prove his word. He looks up toward the Piratain with tears in his eyes.

"Take me to your Emperor in return you will spare his life, as a request I would like to speak with him alone." The Piratain looked at Beckman and then at Tommy.

"I will honor your royal request." His hands left Beckman's neck and he fell to the floor as the Piratain left the office.

Tommy approached Beckman who was still on the floor catching his breath and finally he looked into Tommy's eyes which were full of tears. Beckman lifted his hand to wipe away the tears from his eyes, knowing he is going to die where ever he is going.

"Who are you, why, are you doing this?" Beckman could no longer look into the eyes of this brave child for he has never seen such bravery in one so young looking down at the medallion and notice it was the same one drawn one the paper that was discovered in Tommy's room earlier.

Tommy helped Beckman up and into the chair, having and over whelming feeling he puts his small arms around Troy Beckman who is known to dislike kids he didn't care in the least about them until now as he held this boy he didn't know and wish this wasn't happening, Tommy let go of his neck he took off the medallion and gave it to Beckman for some reason he didn't know but having an over whelming feeling that he knew him. He placed it around his neck.

"I want you to tell the others when they get here what happened. This is for you don't take it off; it will protect you." Tommy said. The Piratain came back into the room, but was now Sheriff Wilson again. Seeing the tears on Tommy's face the Sheriff also lifted his finger to the boys face and touched the tears and suddenly the Sheriff started wailing in pain as all of them watched an image separating from the Sheriff's body separating and other body forms on its own. when the two had finished with transforming Beckman knelt down beside the real Sheriff Wilson feeling his pulse looking up to Duncan he still alive, the other move sitting up he began to rub his neck, on impulse Beckman drew his gun.

"Wait!" The boy said. "What are you?" He asked the life form.

"I am Mobe an Elurain." He said, sounding confused and afraid.

"He's not a Piratain anymore but and Elurain." Seeing the puzzle look on their faces Tommy explained to them what happened years ago on his planet and then telling them about what awaits him on Elura. After he finished talking a Piratain appeared at the door, "Now I must keep my promise" The Piratain grabbed the boy's hand having no love or feeling at all quickly disappeared leaving the most eerie laugh behind.

CHAPTER SEVEN

When they came out of the portal Tommy had created and finding themselves in what looked like a scene out of a movie or from your dreams, for the beauty they saw could not be put into words if you asked one of them to explain what they had seen. There were flowers of every kind and the tree seems to take on a life of there own when they entered into the place they were greeting Tommy in a bowing motion. The birds were nesting in them going about there work joyfully chirping on the way.

Alan and Faith were awe struck forgetting all that had happened to them. After wondering for awhile both; turned to Kevin and seeing a smile gleaming on his face.

"This is what I call home." He raised his hands to what they just seen. "It has been here since I arrived the council thought it would be better to have a place like this on Earth just in case I was not able to make it back or in times of trouble so the Piratains will not be able to track me coming here to help Tommy. This is just a fraction of what Elura looks like."

"But where are we, I feel a little disorientated." Alan asked him.

"We're in a dimensional simulation of Elura, which is virtual reality; it is where I hid the ship so Earth's radar couldn't detect me as I entered the atmosphere. The power source is in side." Leading the way to the ship Kevin tried to answer their questions as best he could so that they will understand how it worked. While they were walking towards the opening of the ship and not realizing Tommy was not with them. Looking up to see the others talking excitingly about the place, walking in the opposite direction he didn't feel like sharing the joy with them for he couldn't forget what had happened to Mason and almost to Faith who has no idea what happened to her early that day. Coming upon a stream he saw a rock he bent down to sit on it and the rock rose to meet him as he sat. He too was in awe of the beauty that surrounded him. Listening to Kevin when he told them the wonder they saw is an actual place on Elura. Then his thoughts started to drift away from their voices. Thinking of how he would like to see his home world and all the sights he only dreamed of seeing, suddenly he noticed the scene had changed he was once again faced with the familiar living room; he stood quickly not sure what to expect. Slowly he scented this was not a dream for he was wearing the same clothes from early that morning, as he sat down feeling the cushion and the softness of the couch, his mother came into the room wearing a jumpsuit it was exactly like the one Kevin wore. He saw her looking so vibrant and refreshed as if nothing had ever happened to her, she continued to walk over to him then kneeling down in front of him. Looking at her he didn't know what to say to her so he looked away instead for the pain of losing her the way he did was still fresh in his heart. Taking her hand she lifted it to try to caress the side of his face.

"Tommy look at me." she gently said slowly he turned to face her.

"Are you real or am I having another daydream?" He asked in an unsure voice.

"I am as real as you want me to be." Tommy brought his arms up to hug her finding them going right threw her wanting to hold her badly and not let go, she saw how hurt he was and wanted so much to touch him again hold him, "Tommy I need to talk to you for it is very important." He wiped his tears from his eyes so he could see her more clearly. Then he suddenly became ashamed of him self, for his father had once told him that crying shows weakness that needs to be strengthened. She smiles, "It's an emotion everybody cries every now and then. It is the way of expressing how we feel, Tommy I don't have much time so I have to be quick about this okay." Nodding his head to show her he understood and kept his mind cleared and on the present moment. She stood up and sat down beside him. "You and Earth are in danger. Every minute you stay in hiding the Piratain Emperor grows restless in finding you. He is at this very minute thinking about destroying Earth, its time to give your self up. When you do this the medallion must not be in your possession when you reach the Emperor. He can't harm you with out it." Cutting her off as he stood up shaking his head. He looked at her in fear.

"Mother they killed you and father because you both didn't have the medallions on, surly he will kill me without it." Grabbing for her hand as it went through, for he was dreadfully afraid now.

"Tommy you are very special, you are not like the other Elurains for it is written down in the ancient scrolls there would be a young Emperor who is not like any other, who has a power of a star child, in time you will understand what I am saying but for right now would you please trust me. Think of it this way Tommy, if Earth is destroyed millions would die when they could have been saved it's your choice and it must be made right now so what would it be." Looking at her and at that moment he begun to understand what his mother had talked about. The determination that welted up in him told what he has to do.

"Okay I'll give myself up." His mother smiled and stepped towards him wanting to caress his face once more then disappeared. Tommy found himself standing right in front of Sheriff Wilson's office. Opening the door watching an officer being lifted off his feet and his throat about to be crushed and hearing the words of the Piratain, he knew at that time what he had to do.

Faith and Alan were so amazed at what Kevin had showed them they forgot all about Tommy and had no idea he was gone until they were inside of the ship Faith noticed that he was not behind her leaving the ships entrance and outside calling his name and not getting any answer, now Faith reentered shouting that Tommy's missing she couldn't find him. She was talking so fast that neither Kevin nor Alan could understand her.

"What happened." said Alan as he shook her hand telling her to calm down?

"Its Tommy he's gone-or have you noticed." Her voice shook as she brought her hands to her lips. Kevin immediately went to a small panel on the wall, placing his hand on it and a computer consul came out.

"GREETINGS IMPERIAL SERVANT, WHAT IS YOUR REQUEST."

"Locate Tommy's life sign's." He said.

"IMPERIAL SERVANT I AM UNABLE TO COMPLY WITH YOUR REQUEST."

"Are you questioning my authority?" He became impatient.

"NO, IMPERIAL SERVANT" The computer said in reply.

"Then locate Tommy's life signs." Kevin turns to the others.

"UNABLE TO COMPLY" The computer answered back. Kevin knew that he had to calm down so he could think.

"Okay, if you can't comply, I ask you why you can't comply." he said calmly through grinding teeth.

"REASON IMPERIAL SERVANT, IT IS AT THE REQUEST OF EMPRESS SHALI."

"You can override her request for she is no longer living." Thinking he had solved the problem and waited for an answer.

"CAN NOT OVERIDE THE EMPRESS REQUEST"

"Then I will override it myself." Touching a button on the consul and a triangular key board popped out of the consul. He started touching the keys the computer had send a little shock to his finger tips, jumping back he quickly removed his hands and continued to step back, watching the computer consul fold back into the wall.

"What's happening?" Alan asked.

"Don't know this has never happened before." Continuing to stare he saw a light starting to take form where the computer consul stood out. Empress Shali stood facing him. 'Empress" Kevin bowed on bended knee.

"Arise Imperial Servant, and welcome Deputy Alan Tate and Faith McCray I have been monitoring your progress and your life signs as well, I would like to say, I grieve with you for the loss of Mason I shared her pain even in death." Kevin looked at her.

"How is it that you are here when the Imperial Council saw yours and Emperor Abel's life signs go out?" she looked at him as he talked.

"We had the Imperial Council enter grate our DNA into the computer systems creating holograms in case of an emergency." Kevin nodding with every word she spoke for on their world they do have the capability to do it. That is how he knew she was for real."

"So the people would still be helped during these trial times."

"Why let the only hope of victory go unprotected, Tommy will be caught."

"Tommy has no choice but to give himself up in exchange for the fate of Earth. If he hadn't gone Earth would have been destroyed and millions would've died. I've been monitoring the Piratain Emperor's orders, for he has two medallions and Tommy's is last one he needs." she stopped and the computer's voice came back.

"EMPRESS, TOMMY'S LIFE SIGNS IS NO LONGER ON EARTH. I''VE LOCATED THE MEDALLION IT IS IN THE POSSESSION OF AGENT TROY BECKMAN, I HAVE PICK UP ON AN ELURAIN

LIFE SIGN" Empress Shari walked over to where Kevin stood as she listened to the computers report.

"Good, make preparations to bring them here."

"YES EMPRESS, LOCKING TRANSPORT SYSTEMS NOW."

Agent Beckman stood up from the chair he sat in and helped the sheriff into it. Wondering what was going to happen next, ever since he was put on the case he has had an interest in the unexplained phenomenon what he saw the Piratain do to him had shocked the living day lights out of him. He had always been in control of a situation and finding out that there is someone more powerful than he makes him think that he should be in front Of a desk the rest of his career, the Elurain got up of the floor looking like he just lost his best friend.

"Where am I?" he said. Beckman started to answer and to drill him with questions that needed to be answered, suddenly the two of them ended up in a place they both didn't know, their vision came in to focus, and he saw four people gathering around them.

"TRANSPORT COMPLETE" Feeling sick Troy Beckman fought to keep the bale down in his stomach.

"Welcome agent Troy Beckman and Mobe I am pleased that you have returned to your normal self after all these years of hate." Mobe the Elurain bowed in homage to the Empress. "Arise you are redeemed and forgiven. It is the Piratain Emperor that shall pay for all that you did against your own people." she turned to Troy Beckman. "Agent Beckman you are the most honored of your kind for you wear the medallion that my son gave you, it is the only one the Piratain Emperor needs protect it as it protects you."

"EMPRESS THERE IS ONLY FIVE OF EARTH MINUTES UNTIL WE LOOSE TOMMY"S LIFE SIGNS."

"Prepare lift off we must stay in contact with his life signs" The ship was taking on another from, and seats came up out of nowhere behind each person, taking the seat Troy Beckman was grateful for it, he didn't know how much longer he could stand on his feet seeing these things transpire before his very own eyes. All those talks about there being aliens form another world he laughed at for he didn't believe that there were such beings. He was taught that we are alone in the universe for there was no evidence to proclaim visitors from other planets. Now he has seen it with his two eyes Troy Beckman was now a true believer in other life forms and their existents. His thoughts wondered a harness came over his head and buckled him in, startled him. He thought it was time to start preparing for the unexpected, for now he needed to sit back and enjoy the ride to where ever they are going, turning to see the Empress.

"Are you going to have to strap in before you fly all over the place." The Empress laughed.

"No, I'm part of the computer I can't go anywhere." she said

"So, your a hologram right."

"In a way, but I am also real, at least I use to be."

"What happened?"

"The Piratain Emperor" had some how gotten a hold of the two medallions we were told to leave behind so that we would be protected from harm. But when he gained the medallions both mine and the Emperor of Elura lives became vulnerable and were killed on Earth." He cut her off.

"You mean the explosion that kill you were caused by a Piratain from far away, how could that be possible." Troy Beckman stopped for a minute. His eyes grew wide. "My God, they can possess our bodies, can't they?" The Empress nodded to answer his question in silence, Troy looked around the ship and seeing two other humans he had not been formally introduced to but now wasn't the place or time to that.

"EMPORESS I AM READY TO LIFT OFF." The computer reported the ships ramp had close with a loud clang indicating the ship was now sealed.

"Proceed then and hurry, we don't have much time."

"AFFIRMITIVE" In the sudden instant there was a rumble through out the ship, and those who were seated began to feel the pressure of the lift off as their heads jerked back on the head rest. The minutes past the computer informed them that they were now outside the Earth's atmosphere. The Empress sensed the three humans had never been outside of Earth's atmosphere and wondered what they were thinking.

"Computer, open the dome." The top of the ship started opening and stars were shining. There were so many of them and everyone gazed up in awe and the excitement welled up in each of them. All of them knew they have a special purpose in life hoping this is the first step towards the unknown goal. Things they took for granted they now appreciated, they are seeing what other people dream about. They are going farther than just to another planet, but to them it is an unexplored section of the universe, the dome had finished opening, it had covered half of the ship.

Troy Beckman wondered if it was safe to have it opened at the rate of speed they were going. The harness came unbuckled allowing them to float to the top of the dome and saw they were approaching the last planet Pluto it only took them a short time to reach it. Amazed in all he was seeing that it felt like a dream perhaps he was still at home dreaming all this up.

"Your kind is so thankful for what they have and I find that very interesting." The Empress said as she came up beside Beckman.

"Well, its because of what we've been though and seen what others haven't, we take life as a gift, that's why we explore things no-one else dared to explore in exploring is knowledge the more we know the better we can make our lives better to live not just for ourselves but for all man kind."

"Why is it hard for your world to obtain peace?" She looked at him in wonder.

"We all have different ideas about how we should live our lives. That is why we fight a lot, we can't come to the same agreement and that causes wars to break out and finally when we are done fighting each other we look back and say to ourselves, this could have been prevented. Sometimes it seems so selfish that we have to make other people live the way we want them to so that we can accomplish a goal that will only glorify ourselves." Seeing the sadness in his eyes, "Sometime I wished so hard that I can make a difference, but find out that it doesn't work that way, you see I work for other peoples ambitions'. Thinking their way is better then mine. That's why humanity is so screwed up because we listen to the wrong people and because of it we suffer for what we've done, and there are time when we gain another step towards the goal of unity and peace, when we reach it, I believe we'll be okay." turning back to her he saw the emotions flowing from her, and the tears welling up in her eyes, wondering if he had offended her in some way.

"No, you just told me that humanity is trying to achieve a goal and if they continue to work towards the goal of unity and piece than they will find it easy to live a life not for them self but for all." They both knew that there was nothing to say at the moment, but to turn there gaze towards the stars and their destination.

Faith was clinging to Alan for dear life as they where looking about at the stars still can't believe they are really out in space. She remembered movies and T.V. shows about the future, she turned to Alan. "We are going where no one on Earth has been before." Alan howled in laughter as Kevin looked at him.

"Why are you laughing?" He explain what Faith had said then telling him about a T.V. show named Star Trek, changing one of the lines of the narrator where he says "Going where no man has gone." Removing the word man and replacing it with one on Earth has." Kevin looked at him,

"That's supposed to be funny?" He turned back to look out at the stars, thinking thoughts of home again and how much of the beauty was still there and untouched by the Piratains. He missed being there. Over the period of month which to Kevin seemed like forever. He hoped for the planet's freedom will succeed to victory and the safety of their young Emperor. Turning away from the dome he touched a button on a small panel then he began to decent to the floor. The computer keyboard came out once again allowing him access to it. His fingers were running fast over the keys and pressed one more key. Kevin forgot to send a message home to let them know they were on there way.

"Waite! What are you doing?" said the Empress.

"Oh, I forgot to send a message to Elura before we left, so I'm sending it now and I coded it so if the Piratains can pick it up they will not know what it says."

"Excellent, then they will be expecting us." She said then turned way as Kevin bow his head gracefully to her.

"EMPRESS WE HAVE REACHED THE WHORMHOLE."

"Prepare to enter and switch on gravity mode."

"COMPLYANCE"

All of them started descending down slowly to the floor just as the way Kevin did. Reaching the floor they returned to their seats so not to be in the way. Immediately the dome began to close and their chair were moving as well. They watched as the dome finished closing and their upper bodies lay leveled with the lower half. Faith was laying there she felt or had a sensation that the whole ship was changing as well. The harness came over them again and then a plastic clear case came over them. Being enclosed into a casket like tomb, Troy felt the panic starting to rise up in him; he squirmed around in his chair. The feeling was getting stronger. His body became aware of it surrounding. Troy Beckman had never in his life felt out of control like he feels now. Hoping the others hadn't noticed yet, he looked towards the others and saw that they were already asleep comfortable. (HOW CAN THEY STAND BEING IN A CLOSED BOX AND NOT PANIC!!?) He thought still struggling to set himself free as the panic started send fear through his body. He tried to scream out, but fear had restricted his throat from any farther sound to come out of it. The Empress watched Troy continued to fight the restrains she saw he was growing tired of fighting giving in to sleep, watching as his body went limp inside of the sleep chambers as he let go of the panic. He slept like the rest of them.

"EMPORESS, THEY ARE NOW IN SLEEPING MODE. IS THERE ANY OTHER REQUEST?"

"YES, there are a few. I would like them all to be monitored while they are sleeping, find out about them through their dreams I would like to know them before we reach Elura. See that no harm comes to them while they are sleeping. When it is time to wake them up I want them to wake-up feeling refreshed and confident about them self."

"UNDERSTOOD EMPRESS"

Empress Shali fades away. Looking like a mother protecting her young from danger, looking at all of them and saw this is her only army and her hope for her son as well, she knew she couldn't enter fear with his destiny.

"Sleep well." Then she was gone.

In the darkness of sleep Troy Beckman found himself walking down a hallway of an old apartment building. He knew this dream very well. Looking side ways he saw his partner was right beside him. His partner pointed to the side of the door and he did what he was told, his partner Rick Baines stood in the front of the door looking like he was about ready to kick it in. but he shouted (F.B.I. OPEN UP!) and at that time a gun went off, blowing a hole through the door and into Rick's chest as he flew backward Troy watched as he fell over dead.

Staying where he was waiting for the suspect to come out of the apartment and start shooting but it hadn't happened that way, instead of an adult a kid came out with a rifle in his hands. Troy Beckman saw him and he flew into an uncontrollable rage and anger he came up behind the kid and disarming him he turned him to face each other and the kid was no more than ten or eleven years of age. Seeing the rage in Troy Beckman's eyes, who picked him up and slamming him hard against the wall and he kept doing that until his back up came in prying his hands off the kid's bloody shirt. He looked at the kid again with cold rage still flowing through his veins Troy saw he had killed the kid for the way his head was rolled into one side of his shoulders unnaturally. He screamed, and then blackness came from everywhere taking the horrible memory back behind closed doors and locked up again. Afraid the rage will return and this time there will be no turning back, it is a part of him self he had always wanted to get rid of. Troy knew he can no longer trust his own emotions because of killing the kid in a blinding rage that is every parent's nightmare, but a terror for him to live with for the rest of his life. To see what he had done to that kid for the rest of his sleeping hours. But this time there was just blackness and a comfortable sleep he would have since the incident eight years earlier. Somewhere in Troy Beckman's mind Tommy is calling out for help. He was telling his captures to let him be. Yet still he pleaded for help kept on in his mind, which he couldn't hear for he was in deep sleep, a dreamless sleep that he is taking advantage of for a while longer.

CHAPTER EIGHT

Tommy had been struggling with the Piratain who was still inside the human he inhabited for his hold was painful as he dragged him to the bridge control room, upon entering the Piratain went proudly to the one in charge of the ship.

"I have the Emperor Child." He gave the commander a sly smile, "Just like you told me to do." The commander looked at him with a look that was meaner than Tommy had ever seen on anyone before the commander didn't have a human body, and the smell made him ill. The Piratain who still held fast on him now shoved Tommy in front of the commander.

"You moron, he's to be brought before the Emperor unharmed."

"What is one lousy push going to do him, we're going to kill him anyway so what the difference." The commander a spiteful look of hate for him, in his mind he is plotting thinking of a way to get the commander into a rage, but decided he would deal with him when the Emperor makes him his right hand. Only then the commander would be in trouble. Making a gurgling sound that was meant to be a silent laugh. The commander looked at Tommy with hate hanging in the air. "Take him to a cell and I want him guarded at all times understood." He barked at the Piratain.

"Yes commander I will do as you ordered." The Piratain grabs Tommy by the arm and yanking him to his feet.

"Before you go, what happened to Mobe?"

"The little rat had transformed him while his feelings where in a vulnerable state." He shook him enjoying seeing Tommy in pain.

"After you are finished with that I want you to contact all the others who are still on this forsaken planet to aboard we have what we came for." consider it done commander." He turns and hurries to get rid of the boy before he does something to him that he will later regret. He ushered Tommy in a booster and took him down to the lower level of the ship where the cells are. Going down a line of them angry shouts and spats of insults came towards Tommy, who was wondering why they hate him so much for he had done nothing to deserve such treatment; then again he knew that he could not reason with the hate which the Piratains thrive on. Soon there was only him and his captor entering another cell block, opening the first cell they came to, he pushed him in and quickly close the door which had no bars to look from then darkness engulfed him as it closed. Tommy immediately stood up going back to the door pounding on it begging them to have some light in there at least, feeling defeated he gave up and went to the corner of the cell and cried, for the first time he truly felt alone and helpless, for there was nothing he could do at the moment to fight back, it had to happened this way. Putting his mind on the memories of good times he's had. He finally slept in the cold darkness. The commander sat back into his seat, with the feeling he had been apart of the emperor's plan of capturing the Emperor child and he was looking forward to presenting to the Emperor the prizes of the child, it had been a long time since he has seen the Emperor smile and he knew that the time has come for the big celebration of their return from Earth. They rode through the wormhole that will take them home, sitting there he began to laugh with glee and pride, with the others smiling along with him. The one who had taken Tommy to his cell sat next to the commander for he had accepted the rank of lieutenant for capturing Tommy, the commander had told him that the Emperor was told of his deed and was rewarded with the rank. The commander also said that the Emperor decided that there will be no one at his right hand of power for there were too many quarrels among the Piratains. At first it didn't sit well with him and. though the commander was lying to him until he heard it from the Emperor's own voice. The commander turned to him.

"You know, I can't wait to see the look on the Imperial Council's face when they find out we have the Emperor Child." The commander's face burned with fury. "They are going to watch him die in the same way his pitiless parents did!" He yelled so all of them could hear him. "Only then will Elura bow down to us. We will become unstoppable." He said with confidence and pride, the Piratains always hated the Elurains for their good deeds and the power they possess. Now they are loosing everything they had worked for all their lives, The Piratain Emperor will rule the planet. The Elurains will be forced to do things his way or die. With a gleam in his eyes the commander ordered the star child be brought to him, for they have reached The Piratain space ship the largest of all the ships they have was now in sight. Tommy was immediately woken up by the unlocking of the door and the light of the ship came pouring in. Lifting up his arm to shield his eyes for they were hurting a Piratain came in grabbing him like the first one did, not allowing him time to get on his feet until they reached cell door. Tommy yelped in pain once more.

"Get up!" said the Piratain. "The commander requested your presence." waiting for him to regain his footing then he was grabbed by the back of his neck and ushered to the commander. Tommy knew the time has come for him to be brought to the Piratain Emperor. Getting out of the booster the first thing he saw was the viewer screen and on it was the red planet or a large ship that stood in orbit around another planet and it was blue he immediately knew it was Elura, for in the direction they were coming from the sun hung from a great distance away, was engulfed with its light, remembering the exact image one the medallion he left in Troy Beckman's hands, standing before the commander who got up from his seat, walking up to the screen.

"Well Emperor Child look into the viewer." He pointed to the red ship, "Isn't it a beautiful sight."

"NO!" he yelled. "It's the ugliest sight I have ever laid eyes on." Tommy said to the commander, who twirled around to face him.

"How dare you to speak of my home that way!" One of the Piratains came behind him and started poking him hard in the side. Tommy knew that if he lashed out on the Piratains allowing his anger to control him all would be lost. The commander saw the anger rising up in the boy, stepping a little closer to him.

"That's it get mad and strike him for poking you." The commander nodded to the one which was behind him. The poking started up again, but this time more of them join in for fun. Tommy told them to stop it then pleaded with them; soon the tears came welling up. The commander was enjoying his suffering, "Strike them, and hit them back." He said those words Tommy allowed himself to calm down as he sat down on the grated floor. He looked up to the commander with determination in his eyes.

"Never, I will not allow myself to become like you. There is nothing you can do to me to make me turn away from my own kind."

"Then, you are a bigger fool then your kind is, for they will loose or have lost the battle. They will watch their only hope die right before their eyes." saying it in a sorrowful voice with the hideous laugh that followed. A Piratain came to the commander.

"Sir the Emperor is waiting for you to arrive with the Emperor Child." Giving the Piratain an angry look he had interrupted his thoughts.

"Fine, prepare for transport, and make it quick the Emperor does not like to wait any longer then he already has."

"Yes sir." The Piratain turned around to go back to his station. The commander took a hold of Tommy's shirt taking him to the same area where he had first arrived on the ship, standing on the platform they immediately faded out from the ship and onto the red ship, after arriving another officer escorted them in to a hug room with only a big chair, which Tommy assumed was the throne room, the floors were so shiny he could see his reflection on it. Going up some steps they came to another Piratain who seemed much bigger than the others. The commander stopped and bowed down on his knee. Tommy thought that it would show politeness if he did to. But decided against it for they are the enemy and he the prisoner, the commander looked at him with such hate that Tommy thought would tear him apart.

"BOW TO THE EMPORER!!" He ordered.

"NO!" Tommy yelled back. The guards kicked at his knees and shoved him forwarded where he fell at the Emperor's feet, getting back up and stood in silence. The Emperor looked at him waving his hands which told the guards to lock him up in a cell for later on until the Piratain Emperor finished celebrating their victory of the Emperor Child's capture. The two guards took Tommy to the only cell near the throne room the room was equipped with furniture for a royal prisoner, one of the guards waved his hand on the wall and instantly the lights came on. The door immediately closed and locked.

Leaving him alone Tommy looked around the room he saw a tray of fresh fruit at a near by table he went over and ate for it had been awhile since he last had something in his stomach. Another door opened and two Elurains came to him bowing down before him arising from the table he looked at the two Elurains and smile as he bent down to help them up. Taking him they took his tattered clothes off of him and bathed him, Tommy putting up a little fuss but it didn't do any good so he allow them to dress him. After they had finished the task they were sent to go they left him alone to finish eating. The clothes he wore were of Elurain white silk the shoes of gold. After he had finished Tommy felt extremely tired so he went to an unusual looking bed. Before his head hit the pillows he was fast asleep. While Tommy slept the door came into unlocked position the door opened. The Piratain Emperor stood over his sleeping form. Hostility and rage came from the Piratain Emperor as he watched Tommy sleep, tossing and turning the Emperor realized that he was about to wake the Emperor child from his slumber, he saw it was not the right time to get the medallion from him, and knew that Tommy will give it to him of his own free will, stepping out of the room he knew that he must gain the trust of the Emperor child, turning to the guards who were guarding both sides of the door.

"I want to allow the star child to roam the palace let him go anywhere he wishes. If anyone touches him or to make a sly remarks or try to harm him in anyway I want them brought to me is that clear." Giving them a stern look, the two guards nodded their heads in unison, taking their orders without question. The Piratain Emperor turned and left, the two guards looked at each other in questioning silence. Ever since Tommy's arrival he saw the child for the first time, and knew that there was potential in him and if he could win him over to their side then the war would be easily be won in their favor. The Piratain Emperor had smiled at the treachery of his plan that formed in his mind when he saw Tommy's refusal not to bow down to him. (He would make a fine and loyal son to him. He knew taking his life would be meaningless and the child could be used for a better purpose) He thought when he addressed the same message to the messenger to take to the people. Sitting on his throne all he could do is watch the plan being played without Tommy's suspicions? He would be too busy with being treated with royalty like a true Emperor is supposed to be treated. The Piratain Emperor patted himself on the back; he didn't trust anyone else about what he is up to.

Tommy was still sleeping thrashing his arms and legs, the desperate cries in slow moaning pleading for someone to help him. Waking suddenly; with a silent scream in his throat about ready to bellow out. Sitting up in the bed sweat came down and dripped under his chin as he brought his hands up to wipe it off. Continuing to sit on the bed his thoughts went back to what Kevin had said that his powers that not all of it came from the medallion and in just minutes after waking up from seeing his mother telling him the same thing except that the Emperor had his big hands around her throat and after he saw her lifeless body being thrown away like trash The Piratain Emperor came after him with the same frisky fury he has seen so many times now that he is beginning to grow accustom to seeing it everywhere they took him it no longer frighten him. Tommy decided to stop contemplating about his situation but to take the opportunity to explore his room which there wasn't much to see. Confined to a room was a little better than being in a cold dark prison cell any day. Running his hand over the flowers that stood in the same place where the unusual best tasting fruit he'd ever had. He continued to touch the flowers and noticed that they move where ever he waved his hand. There was much he needed to learn so he sat down to think. Looking about the room searching for nothing in particular, he laid his eyes on a funny looking sculpture, having no idea what it was suppose to be. He scooted his chair around so that he would be facing the object; settling himself in the chair again so he was comfortable steadying his gaze on the sculpture he began to feel the familiar tingling inside his head and at once the sculpture rose from its resting place, as Tommy began to will it to him, the sculpture slowly came to him. Opening his hands he released the sculpture with his mind, sailing now he understood what Kevin and his mother have said about him was true. Suddenly the door he had came through when he first arrived opened slowly and the Emperor saw that he was now awake and was holding an Elurain sculpture. Tommy looked at him with fear in his eyes wondering what the Piratain Emperor was going to do with him, now that he was there. Tommy looked at him he wondered what his intentions were at the moment. Still holding the sculpture he went back to the place next to the bed and put it carefully down. Then he faced the Piratain Emperor.

"Ah, you're up. I hoped that your had a good rest." He said in a pleasant tone of voice.

"I can't complain. It was okay I guess." He looked down at the floor so that he would not have to look into those terrible eyes. The Piratain Emperor came into the room not so far, he did not want to frighten the star child any farther.

"I apologize for the way you were treated when you got here I assure you that it will not happen again here." Giving a smile as he watched Tommy look up. He made a slight smile of his own not sure it he should trust the word of his capture. You are welcomed to go anywhere you wish to go. You are no longer a prisoner but a guest of honor in the highest regard. For you is Emperor of Elura." The Piratain Emperor made it known that he was a guest Tommy didn't know how to react to it but to graciously except.

"Thank you, I'll just stay here for awhile longer if that is okay."

"Sure, that will be okay." The Piratain Emperor turned and left him a lone. Leaving the door opened, as the Piratain Emperor left Tommy went to the door and closed it again. He noticed the guards did not pay him any mind. His thoughts turned back to his new found power, knowing that he must not let anyone else know he has to continue to practice harnessing it and to find out what other things he can do if he puts his mind to it. The Piratain Emperor one of his subjects came running to his side.

"My lord, we have detected an Elurain ship just coming out light speed not far from here. My guess is that they are heading for the planet. What course of action do you want us to take?" The Emperor stopped and thought for a minute.

"Do nothing allow them to pass."

"Yes, my lord." He took off running again. Watching him go, the Emperor thought if he did the right thing or should he have the ship destroyed. Shrugging his shoulders and smiled to him self. (I already got what I need it's just a matter of time for me to take possession of the medallion.) He thought as he started resuming his walk again.

Inside the room Tommy thought to try something else, he wondered if he would be able to read the filthy minds of the Piratains, going to the door where he knew the two guards stood at his door. He concentrated one of them his mind tingled as he pressed hard soon he began to here things in one of the guards mind not only can he here what the other thought but feel the pride and doubt among others feelings Tommy couldn't understand, the madding rage that is constantly there needing to be satisfied. Unable to bear being inside the Piratains' mind so he with drew from it. Staggering backwards he fell on his rump and his teeth bit down on his tongue. The pain went through him, clapping his mouth so that he would not let out a scream to alarm the guards. A few minutes have past by and Tommy lifted his hand away and the pain had subsided only the throbbing remained. Getting up from the floor he stood up taking mental notes to beware of there thoughts only to use the ability when it was necessary to. He became bored so he decided to take the Piratain Emperor's word. Going to the door he looked out saw the two guards still standing there taking the courage to step out of the room and stood in front of the guards who still paid him no mind, which to Tommy looked funny after all he's been told about the Piratains who always takes a look at their enemy and never taking their eyes off of them.

"I would like to go somewhere to look out at Elura or at the stars?" He said bravely looking into one of them eyes.

"Right this way please." He follows the guards to the observation room. He was alone there as well the room does not look like it had been used that much during the war or battle which is nearing its end after what others have told him that the battle started long before he was born. He thought if only there was a simple way out of this war, but he had searched thoughtfully and desperately for a way to end all the nonsense. Tommy didn't not like thoughts of that so he just allow his mind wonder he looked at the planet which caught his gaze in awesome beauty he saw the planet was also like the one in the medallion with light blue mixed in the white milky stuff he thought would be clouds. He began to search the stars for Earth he knew it would be to far away to see. He scanned the darkness of space he noticed a ship was slowly going to Elura. Turning around he had to make sure the guards would not notice what he was going to do. Seeing them looking the other way he turned to see the ship still moving to their destination. Settling his thoughts he projected his mind out. Soon he began to get closer the ship. Entering it he recognized both Faith and Alan standing near Kevin and talking about something that he really didn't know for he only made out a few words. He turned around, and was the man whose name was Troy Beckman. Still wearing the medallion, Tommy thought that the medallion was in danger of being discovered. He became afraid that he pushed harder to reach Agent Beckman's mind. Finding out he could not reach him, or that he was either going about the wrong way in doing it. Not caring what the guards think he closed has eyes and allowed his mind to roam free out side the ship. Now he reentered the ship through the dome.

"Agent Beckman, can you hear me." Tommy saw Agent Beckman looking about wondering where the sound came from. "This is Tommy I'm inside of you head. Talk to me with your thoughts." Troy Beckman looked up in surprise telling everyone one the ship that Tommy was there.

"Tommy is that really you?"

"Yes it is. Go to the dome and look out." Agent Beckman went to the dome and there was the red ship.

"I am there in the red ship." Tommy saw Agent Beckman looking out of the dome although the Elurain ship was to far away, Tommy could since his presences on the ship. "Tell the others that I am okay for now and waiting for the right time for me to join all of you once again." Tommy then pulled out of Troy Beckman's mind and saw back in the observation deck. He looked to see if the Piratain guards noticed anything funny while he was inside the agent's mind. Seeing them in the same position they were before. Turning away from the window he started out of the room. The guards fell in right beside him keeping the same pace Tommy walked as they went back to the room where he was put before. He saw there was more fruit on the table upon entering. Looking at it he thought they were fattening him up for some reason or another. Decided he was not hungry at all, but returned to the chair and focused on the Piratain Emperor's mind to see what his plans are about and what they are going to do with him. Searching through the ship he found the Piratain Emperor standing on a deck. Watching the Elurains being beaten on for fun and games Tommy found the scene very repulsive he was about to with draw as he heard the Piratain Emperor. Telling the Elurains his plans of how he was going to get the medallion and make Tommy his son. Telling them that Empress Shali didn't deserve a son such as Tommy and as the Emperor of Elura was long since been dead and they might as well give up and join the winning team. Tommy drew out immediately for he became very upset with the way they where treating his people and degrading them into nothing. They were stripping them of all their dignity and self respect. Tommy decides he would no longer play out this game the Piratain Emperor had devised. When he did come for the medallion he will see that Tommy didn't have it. Still the outcome of this war remains unknown.

CHAPTER NINE

When they had awakened from their sleep the computer told them that they were in distance of the Piratain ship they had detected them. Everyone was hoping they would not be fired upon for the Elurain ship didn't carry weapons to fire back. Troy Beckman sat up from the sleep chamber he was in having no idea how long they had been asleep in those things which he began to be very much what they reminded him of a time when he was trapped inside a building that had a bomb in it was the only one they are, too says he began racing towards the door of the building the bomb went off and he was caught underneath a lot of rubble from the explosion. He thought he would die, but after a few hours the rescue team had found him barely alive, He quickly got off it and roamed around watching Kevin at work; not sure of what he was doing but knew that everything was better than setting in that chair.

"This is very unusual." Kevin said as Beckman approached him.

"What is?" He said.

"The Piratains usually would fire their weapons when an Elurain ship passes them, but this time they were letting us pass without any casualties."

"Well maybe they already got what they came to Earth for; that would be Tommy."

"No, what the Piratain Emperor wants is what you got around your neck. Maybe the Emperor doesn't know that Tommy does not have the medallion, if that is the case we could consider ourselves lucky." Kevin said as he continues typing on the keyboard. When he had finished he noticed Beckman was looking around the ship. "What's wrong?" Kevin was concerned.

"It's Tommy; I can hear him up here." Pointing to his head and stopped to listen even more intently he looked up and smiled. He went to the dome which was already opened when they had awakened. He saw the red ship the nodded and turned around to face the others who were unsure of what was happening to him.

"Great, it looks like that Agent Beckman just when off the deep end never to return." He smiled at Faith who did not like his punch line at all. Giving him a grim look that told him to keep his commits to himself for he was not helping matters much. Alan winced at it. "Sorry bad joke." That was the first time that Faith had ever given anyone that kind of look that she knew of.

"Tommy said to tell all of you that he was okay at the moment and is waiting for the right time to rejoin us again." Troy smiled to reassure them that he was not crazy.

"Well that just confirms what I said earlier." Beckman nodded in agreement with him.

"What is that?" Alan stood closer to Faith.

"It means that the Piratain Emperor does not know yet about the medallion being gone." Beckman's smile suddenly when into a worry some frown. "But when he finds out all hell will break loose." Everyone was silent for a few minutes; the computer told them they are within transporting range to the planet. After the computer had finished informing them the Empress Shali reappeared to them once again.

"I just wanted to say thank you for coming all this way from Earth to help in any way possible. My only wish I have for each of you is to see Elura the way it use to be, now there are only a few places left untouched by the destruction that Piratains have done." Agent Beckman cut her off.

"Empress our main concern right now is to see the rest of the battle through together and I speak for all of us." turning to look at the others to see if the agree with him.

"I'm with you all the way Empress." Alan said.

"That goes for me too." Faith stood her ground firmly as the others watched in astonished by her courage. Faith had also surprised herself in the way she had been acting it was unlike her and she knew that.

"Let me say that all of you." She pointed to the three humans "Were monitored during your sleep I had given each of you what you will need to endure the pains you will be going through. Faith McCray I found that you lacked Joy so we gave you some. Alan Tate you lacked patience with your self that is where you will draw your strength." The she turned to Agent Beckman, "You Troy Beckman is the main key to the elect. You lacked the most important ingredient that all life should be allowed to have no matter what you have done in the past must be let go before you embark onto the planet. Let go of the anger towards wrong doers. For it is time for you to use the gift that all possess we could not give you, but deep inside you is the gift of love. Remove all hate now or it will over take you." Troy Beckman for the first time broke down and cried for he knew the Empress saw the horror of his dreams that had plagued him for so long. He felt he was unworthy to live his life in love for the things he had done years before. He looked into the eyes of the Empress which were filled with love and compassion for him.

"Yes, I will leave hate behind for good." At that moment Beckman's eyes were no longer hard from the years of hate and he felt the heaviness of his chest being lifted from him. The love came over him like a cleansing tidal wave.

"EMPRESS IT IS TIME FOR TRANSPORT. WHAT IS YOUR REQUEST?"

"Proceed as planned." She said and turned to all of them. "As you go I will not be there, so go in my peace and love and welcome to Elura." She said as the three of the quickly disappeared. With Kevin and Mobe remaining on board the ship.

"What do we do from here your highness?" Kevin asked. The Empress looked at him and though a moment.

"I think it is time that we pay the Piratain Emperor a visit." Kevin nodded in agreement.

"Computer, reverse course to the Piratain red ship"

"REVERSING THUSTERS AND COURSE LAY IN IMPIREAL SERVANT."

"Mobe, I want you to remain on the ship, no matter what happens from here on out you do not leave here."

"Understood Empress I will stay here." He was thankful that he would not have to face the Piratains again.

"Computer" The Empress said.

"YES EMPRESS, WHAT IS YOUR REQUEST?"

"Switch to emergency mode. If there is any sign of trouble I want you to liftoff and return to the planet.

"SWITCHING TO EMERGENCY MODE, YOUR REQUEST IS ON STAND BY EMPRESS" She turned to Kevin

"Now we wait." Crossing her arms she turned to look out at the red ship.

"EMPRESS, WE ARE WITHIN RANGE OF THEIR COMMUNICATION SENARS. WHAT IS YOU REQUEST?"

"Good, send a request to aboard, don't tell them who. I want that to be a surprise for the Emperor."

"AFFIRMITIVE" they waited for an answer. "REQUEST APPROVED, PREPARING DOCKING PROCEEDURES."

"Computer can you replicate a device to fit my DNA form?"

"AFFIRMITIVE" after a few minutes a device materialized on a small platform nest to the console. Kevin went over picking it up, he then placed it on the inside of his wrist.

"DOCKING NOW" there was a familiar hiss as the air filled the small tunnel which lead to the docking bay filled with all types of crafts. Leaving the ship the Empress gave Mobe a look that told him to close and lock the hatch after they were off the tunnel. Mobe nodded his head in understanding her silent message. Two armed Piratain guards were waiting for them, but had no idea who it was. When they saw the Empress they fled from their post to tell the Emperor who had just came on board. Leaving them unguarded the Empress merely enjoyed seeing the guards look frighten for the first time ever since she had known them had never seen them scared before. As they went up a flight of stairs they could hear the Piratain Emperor going into a range pushing the guards around.

"Emperor, its Empress Shali she is still alive!" Said one of the guards who were shaking all over Kevin and the Empress entered to see the other guard been thrown across the room. The Piratain Emperor faced them.

"Well Empress Shali and her Imperial Servant. What a nice surprise to see you both again so soon." He said trying to control the rage that roared within him.

"I thought it would be it's time we had a little talk since I couldn't do it a long time ago."

"I have to wonder what kind of talk that would be?" Seeing her as he grabbed the railing so he wouldn't fall; due to shock of seeing her again standing right in front of him. "After all we are enemies. What could we possibly have to talk about?" Then it hit him. "Oh, you would like to talk about my prize that you want to take away from me. Well let me say you'll never see him again." He turned to one of the guards in disgust.

"BRING ME THE STAR CHILD NOW!" The guard got up to the floor and went to retrieve him.

"Yes Tommy is on my list of things to talk to you about." She said coldly. "But I'm afraid he is in no use to you." The Piratain Emperor stood up firmly.

"DO YOU TAKE ME A FOOL?" Tommy was brought in seeing his mother he jumped for joy but then stopped for he knew the truth she did die. Wondering how it is that she was here. Seeing him she quickly shook her head not to say anything out loud.

"I'm here to ask you to first release my son to surrender and end this war except defeat."

"NEVER, I HAVE THE LAST MEDALLION IN MY POSSESSION AND YOU THINK I'M GOING TO LISTEN TO YOU!" He flew in a range of hatred for her. "I HAD YOU KILLED AND I WILL TRY AGAIN." He held his hand out immediately a guard place to weapon in it. The Piratain Emperor pointed it at her and then fired.

"NO!" Tommy yelled as he saw the weapon dislodge a laser beam towards his mother and it went right through her. She stood in the same place not budging. The Piratain Emperor ordered all of them to aim and shoot both Kevin and the Empress. As they started firing Kevin fell to the ground and the device gave way from his wrist. Suddenly a blinding white light surrounded Kevin he then vanished like he was ever there. Leaving the device behind, the Emperor raised his right hand signaling a cease fire. The Empress continued to stand there as the Piratain Emperor walks over to where the device had stopped spinning around. Bending down he picked it up recognizing what it was he looked at the Empress.

"Very clever, you are after all dead and before you died you had you DNA intergraded into the ships computer." "Go to the ship and destroy it." He said to the guards not taking his eyes off of the Empress.

"The ship is gone my lord." One of the guards said over a loud intercom.

"What!" He looked at the Empress in the eyes the Piratain Emperor threw the device down on the ground and mashing it with his heel. The Empress faded away with the look of disappointment on her face.

"Why" Tommy yelled out with shear courage coming from his voice that it made the Piratain Emperor jump a little. "As if killing her once was not enough for you, so you killed her again and in the process you killed my Imperial Servant Kevin." Standing there he knew there was no redemption for what the Piratain Emperor did. Tommy now sees him as nothing but a pure greedy and very evil monster. He looked at the Piratain Emperor with clarity in his eyes. "You will never be satisfied, for now you will think that you have won but I will destroy you in a way when you least expect it." The Piratain Emperor saw that there was no son in his future.

"Give me your medallion so that I can end you life as well." Tommy just looked at him and smiled. "Come on hand it over you rut!"

"You will never have my medallion. It is not yours to take." The Piratain Emperor was getting impatient.

"Search him!" He ordered. As the Puritan guards laid hands on Tommy, he looked at one of them and suddenly the guard flew across the room with an impact force can knock a human out of breath and unconscious. "How did that happen?" He said to the other guard who stood there dumbstruck. Shrugging his shoulders told the Piratain Emperor that he didn't know.

"As I said you'll never have my medallion. I know who I am now and it's time for me to start acting like an Elurain Emperor." The Piratain Emperor stepped forward and backhanded Tommy hard, the force of the blow knocked him to the floor he felt the sting in his face and a taste of blood in his mouth. His hand to what the corner of his mouth and saw the blood.

"Get him out of my sight so I can think straight!" The Emperor demanded. Both of the guards grabbed Tommy at once and immediately they were howling in pain. The Emperor turned to them again. "Now what" He yelled and saw the bewilderment and the guard's eyes.

"He burned us somehow." One of them said.

"If you want me out Emperor your going to have to remove me you're self." Tommy saw the look of fright on his face. "What's the matter are you scared of a 10-year-old boy?" Tommy laughed as he continued to giggle he didn't realize that there was someone behind him until it was too late, suddenly everything went dark when he didn't feel the blow that was directed to the head. He fell to the floor both guards grabbed his arms and drag him back to the room. The Emperor was pondering the question of how Tommy could do those things. For there is no one on Elura with those abilities which he saw the child do. Shaking head he refused to believe that Tommy was the star child the savior of Elura. For the scrolls were written a long time ago. To the Emperor it sounded crazy to believe in what those prophets of old had warned Elura about a great battle and of a child that is like no other will save them from destruction. He waved it off as nothing more than an old tale. The Emperor continued to go about his business to find out where the last medallion could be. Barking orders for the planet to be scanned again for it had to be somewhere down there. He will be well on his way in becoming the Emperor of Elura. He laughed the way Tommy did but with, but with hate and greed seeping through his hideous laughter.

Mobe sat in his seat he sat in it during the whole journey. Suddenly the Empress reappeared startling him.

"Computer, take us to Elura at once there must not be a delay."

"AFFIRMATIVE EMPRESS" Mobe sat quietly for a while as he saw the Empress was in distress.

"So Kevin didn't make it my Lord?" she turned to Mobe.

"No, Mobe he was killed the same way that they had killed me and the Emperor Abel. I'm afraid that I may have put Tommy in danger as well." She did not look at him for she did not want him to loss his hope for victory. For the only thing that is keeping Elura alive at the moment was hope.

Tommy lay on the floor of the royal prison. He dreamed of Kevin and of his mother, in the dream they had showed him things that he could do with his powers. He was so excited for he was finally beginning to understand and knowing more about his destiny. He listened to what they were saying and teaching him the final lesson of Love and Peace so he would be able to bring Elura back to the state of harmony with one another.

Now that everything rests on his shoulders, and now he has accepted himself as Emperor He must now reclaim the family throne. He was told about the beginning of how this war had started. His mother told him that the Piratain Emperor was his father's brother who became greedy and wanted to rule all of Elura, so he planed to have them killed for he had killed their Father. When his plans had failed his father and the Council had banished him from the planet never to return, and he took a lot of its citizens with him bye spreading lies about the Elurain Emperor Abel and saying that is was his choice to leave Elura. No one knew about the plot to kill the Emperor or about the secrets to over throw the throne him self. Tommy knew that the evil must be completely destroyed in order for him to bring Elura to where they once were so that his people can enjoy life once more.

CHAPTER TEN

Upon being transported down to the surface of the planet Faith, Alan, and Troy gasped at what they saw. They were standing in the middle of a platform which has the symbol of the medallion that Troy was wearing around his neck. They stood there two guards came towards them, not that none of them had noticed at the time for they were still admiring the great building which was all made out of crystal or glass it was hard for them to tell and the sun was shining from different angles of the building. Their eyes adjusted to the light there was smoke coming up from the hills just outside of the complex and all their joy and quickly disappeared as they came back to their senses. Faith saw the guards first and introduced themselves to the guards.

"Welcome to Elura Emperor Abel is expecting you." Said one of the guards who was well built and just a little taller than Troy. Both guards bowed to them which were one of the customs they had on Elura.

"What is this place?" asked Alan as he continued to allow his eyes to wonder; seeing so many computer consoles and people going about their business.

"It's the Central Command Post and there are more like it all over the planet. All of the outposts are in constant contact for we do not have the capability to keep the Piratains out of our atmosphere." The guard pointed to the hills. "They almost tried to destroy this command center. If we didn't have our shields up to protect us we would not be here right now."

"Is that what is surrounding the planet at this time?" said Faith.

"No, what you saw was a generated shield that constantly keeps the air of our planet from being polluted for the effects of the war that is going on. Anything the Piratains throw into our atmosphere that could cause harm to our air would not be able to enter; it is automatically destroyed once the shield sensor picks it up and identifies it." Troy nodded his head in agreement.

"I heard about their weapon capabilities."

"We cannot delay another minute the Emperor wants all of you to join him in the conference hall along with the Imperial Council." They followed the guards and kept up with their pace. Cutting through the command center for a faster way to the conference hall and watch as the Elurain people looked their way in hopes that in some way they would be of some help to them. Troy was walking beside a guard as he continued to talk with them Faith and Alan followed behind them as the second guard brought the rear. The group came to a stop in front of a metal door and the guard had pressed his hand against a panel and the door immediately opened and stepped inside. Troy thought it was some kind of elevator for the stood there for no more than a split second. The door opened into a huge room which had nothing but a long table with high back chairs around it was a computer consul at the head of the table. The two guards ushered them in and left. They heard a loud swooshing sound like that of a whirl wind and a man dressed up in the same kind of uniform the Empress had worn looked out of the window seeing the smoke still rising in the distance he turns away from the view he saw his guests had arrived safely on the planet he greeted them and offered them the seats at the head of the table.

"You are our most honored guests here on Elura for you have brought back the last medallion safely to us." He said with a smile on his face. Faith went to the window seeing that they were high above the ground and she quickly backed away. The man looked at her with concern. "Is everything alright?" His thick eyebrows went down to from a V shape just above his nose. At that instant he looked just like Tommy but an older version of him. Suddenly they all knew he was the Emperor Abel for he had the same features and qualities his son has and his body was well muscular built and has a since of love and compassion for his people and the well being for his guests. Faith thought that if there was any given chance that he would trade places with Tommy in a heartbeat. (I guess we all would.) She thought as she regained her wits about her.

"I'm just not used to being up so high." She smiled to reassure him that it is nothing to be concerned about.

"Very well then please be seated all of you." He gestured with his hand towards the head of the table. "We are about ready to start the meeting."

They sat down and they Imperial Council walked quietly and sat around the table as well. All was silent until the last member hurried to take a seat. Emperor Abel stood staring out the window again deep in thought and yet worried about their next move. He turned away from the window.

"Where there any survivors from the Piratains last attack?" A woman got up ready to give her report when the door opened and an Elurain who seems to be a commander burst into the room went straight to the Emperor he bowed before him and started to talk fast in a tone which no one else could hear him. When he finished the Emperor grabbed the end of the table and slowly sat down into his chair. With a grave look on his face told everyone in the room that something terrible has happened and will be inform of the few in just minutes? The commander had said something to him the Emperor just shook his head the Elurain turned and left without say another word or looking at anyone in the room. The woman waited to see if the Emperor wanted to hear her report. From the looks of her Troy knew that the Emperor would not bare any more bad news and yet he was surprised when he spoke. "I have just received word that the Empress Shali had tried an attempt to talk to the Piratain Emperor in hopes they could reach an agreement of some sort. In the process the Piratain Emperor became enraged and killed the Imperial Servant Kevin." All at once talk broke out among them then out of desperation another Elurain stood and address the council.

"Emperor, I understand you grief for all those who have died in the cost of freedom from the Piratains, How many more of us have to die before this whole thing is over with. The people of Elura are growing weaker as the days go by hoping the star child would end the war quickly before there is no one around for him to rule over." Emperor Abel stood once again.

"If the people give up then we might as well surrender to the Piratains and I will not let that happen. We have to pull together and devise a plan that will hold until such time Tommy reclaims the throne. It is all up to him, all we can do is to keep the people from giving up." He turned to the three humans who were listening intently. "I have forgotten about the one thing we do have and that is the last medallion." motioning for Troy Beckman to stand and the other two as well.

"Maybe if the people knew that we have it then their hope will be strengthen and making them stronger to want to hold out and not give up." The Elurain also stood up nodding his head in agreement with the Emperor.

"But how long will that last, even if they knew will they continue to doubt?" The council agreed with him for they themselves were in doubt as well.

"I know that this is not my place to speak but if Emperor Abel and the council would allow me. I may have something that may help." Troy looked at the Emperor seeming to think for an answer. The Emperor gestured for Troy to have the floor.

"Ever since I had met Tommy, at the time I thought I would die at the hands of a Piratain. When he came into the building where I and a few others of my kind were, Tommy had stopped them from killing all of us. When he had given me the medallion to keep safe for him, I knew that he was giving himself up so Earth would not be destroyed. For the first time in my life I have never seen such courage in one so small. What I saw in his eyes was love for life no matter what life form it was. It was at that moment I felt like I had a chance to help save a life instead of taking it. When we were on our way here the Empress spoke of love and compassion and peace along with all the other emotions that tie in with them were becoming clear to me. Yet when I hear that your people can do nothing more than hope, but there is more that you can do. You can use your emotions of love joy and peace as a weapon again the Piratains fleet." An Elurain interjected Cutting Troy off.

"This is none since, how could we use our emotions as weapons without the Piratains knowing our every step." The council voiced their agreement with her. He held up his hands in protest.

"Let me ask you this." He challenged her

"Do the Piratains have the capability to read your minds?"

"No," she answered

"What I am trying to point out to you here is Tommy has the capability and also has the power to do many more things, the reason why I know this is because he and I can talk with our minds without the Piratains knowing about what we are saying. If what I am going to say is true then there is a good chance this war will come to an end soon, but it will involve the people of Elura as well." Troy looked around the room to see if anyone will object to it. "What I would like to suggest is getting all the people to think positive emotions and having faith Tommy will hear their thoughts then he will be able to draw strength from them and be more determine to fight the Piratains for the good and well being of his people?" Troy then sat down again, Faith leaned over towards him.

"Where did you get all that from?" Troy shrugged his shoulders for he did not know where he got it from it had shocked the dickens out of him.

"I guess it was there all this time and I just realized it would be a good way to help them to fight for their cause instead of sitting on my butt twiddling my thumbs." Faith laughed softly to herself. The council talked for a while about Troy's suggestion and came to the decision that it was worth a try. Only then did Troy allow himself some mental rest and to continue to think of ways they could use the power of their emotions. The Emperor Abel was pleased with the council for the first time they seem to be working together instead of arguing about their options. When they were finished talking all became quite. The Elurain girl stood to give her answer on their decision.

"We have reached an agreement on this proposal and would like to get this plan under way as soon as possible." She said addressing the Emperor who was pleased and began asking for the rest of the reports. Soon the meeting was over and everyone left in an urgent rush to get the message out to the Central Command Posts so the Imperial servants can reach the nearby cities for what the human said was to do it without allowing the Piratains to know what they are up to. Soon all Elura will put their thoughts to work against the evil Emperor their quest for peace will resound throughout the war until it is over.

Troy Beckman tried to reach Tommy's thoughts, but got no answer. He kept trying until his head was aching from thinking too hard. He didn't know Tommy was knocked out laying on the floor unconscious unable to hear him. Emperor Abel rejoined them after overseeing the task gets out okay.

"Did you get to him?"

"No," Troy said in frustration. "But I'll keep trying." With a smile on his face told the Emperor he was not a person who gives up easily. Faith stood up from a very nice comfortable chair for it vibrates automatically when you sit in it. She was getting tired and felt that there should be something for her to do while they waited to hear from Tommy.

"Is there anything I can do to help, I'll go crazy if I'm not given something to do soon." Emperor Abel looked at her then his eyes sparkled.

"As a matter of fact there is something all of you need to do." He paused for a few minutes. "We need to teach you how to use the medallions Kevin had given you. Come with me." The Emperor beckoned them to follow him. Leading them into a serious of rooms he bought them to a stop and opened the last door. "This room has not been used in a long time; the last time was when Tommy was born." The lights came on as the Emperor touched the wall. Walking in they saw nothing at first until he ordered the computer to activate the Medallion program. Objects appeared on some tables. "Here is where we start. The medallions can only be used to save your selves from evil. Your thoughts of peace and love and all the others emotions, never use it out of anger or hostility. The effects would be disastrous for the one who is wearing them. They are a living organism which monitors you heart beat and vital signs. When joining your thoughts with the medallion you will be surprised in what you can do." He went over to the table and picked up a ball with spikes coming out of them on the upper half of it. Instructing them to clear their minds and focus on their positive emotions, as they did, he watching their medallions became bright with colors. He walked over to another table which had a rounded hole in the middle. Taking the ball and placed it inside the hole and then the hole closed up the room began to hum and the vibrations became more intense to the point where they could feel it with their bodies. All at once the table where the ball had been lifted off the ground, the three of them where focusing on the table at the same time. Breaking their concentration the table fell to the floor with a loud bang. "Good now try to," Suddenly there was a loud howling scream broke through the air like a thunderous roar cutting off the Emperor's words. Troy Beckman was on his knees screaming in pain both Faith and Alan bent down to hold him down for his arms and legs were thrashing all over the place and they thought that he might hurt himself without knowing it. The screaming had stopped for a while, but then it started up again it was like he was being tortured by an unknown being. Faith could not stand it any longer clapping her hands over her ears she got up from the floor and ran out of the room not bothering to look back to see if Troy was still thrashing about like a crazy man.

"What is happening to him?" Alan said, yelling over the humming.

"I don't know?" The Emperor yelled back. Stopping the program he turned to them wanting to help. "Computer medical emergency we need help."

"MEDICAL TEAM IS ON THE WAY." After a short while Troy Beckman went limp and was quietly sleeping as if nothing happened at all.

"Will he be okay?" He looked at the Emperor for reassurance.

"I think so, but we need to find out what happened to him when he wakes up." Alan shook his head in agreement without taking his eyes off Troy he was not sure whether or not if he would go back to screaming and thrashing. Two Elurains came in to the room with a hover bed coming in behind them. They lifted him off the floor and onto the bed as an invisible restraint went over his body just in case he starts thrashing again. The hover bed left the room with on one attending to it. Emperor Abel excused himself and left with the two Elurains at his side. Alan looked around the room and did not see where Faith had gone. At the time he was concerned about Troy's dilemma. Getting up he left the room and went searching for her. He found himself back into the main room when they had first arrived. The Elurains were busy with their duties, wondering if they ever take a coffee break every now and then. Since Faith was nowhere to be found he decided to go exploring on his own, after all he did want time to himself to think about his relationship with Faith. He was not sure that it would be a good time to really to get into loving her for he did not want to lose her the way he had lost his wife by not thinking right about safety. He no longer blames himself, but still knew there was something he could have done to prevent her from being killed. Alan would be well on his guard to make sure it would not happen to Faith.

Upon entering another room which was even larger than the one where they had the Imperial meeting with the council it was set like a lounge and divided into several sections a relaxation unit, a game room unit and a dining room unit. As he looked around he saw Faith in the dining room unit sitting at a table with a cup in her hand, looking down into whatever liquid the cup was holding not realizing Alan was watching her. He slowly walks over to the table.

"May I join you?" Uncertain what she will say.

"Of course, you are always welcome to sit at my table any day." Smiling she was thankful to have his company. Alan pulled out a chair and sat in it.

"So, what happened back there?" He asked. Looking at her to see if he could figure it out, but her face was concealed by whatever she was thinking. For Alan had thought she did not want to discuss it.

"Well, I have freaked out before, but this feeling was something I have in my whole life ever experienced. I was just over whelmed by the fact all three of us lifted a table off the ground without touching it. The thing with agent Beckman, talking about seeing a horror movie. Just see him all wretched up in pain. I guess a just kind of lost it, but I am feeling better now. How is he doing?"

"After you left he passed out from excursion and then two Elurains came and took him away. That was the last I have seen of him." Alan quickly changed the subject and they were talking about their own lives Alan want to know more about her before he decides to go ahead with the relationship without any regrets right now they needed time to themselves to forget their present situation at the moment.

Troy woke up from his sleep and seeing an Elurain dabbing his stomach with some kind of solution which gave out a cool sensation. Bringing his hand up to his neck he could still feel the medallion around his neck. Just before all the pain came into his body he was thinking about the medallion and why no one else on Elura was wearing them. The Elurain had finished with what she was doing and left the room. Troy thought he was alone so he started to get up and finding that he was being restrained.

"Are you okay?" said the voice in the dark room.

"I'm fine would like to sit up though." Immediately the restraints disappeared and he was able to move freely.

"Do you know what happened to you?" Troy answered back with a nod of his head. "Can you explain?"

"Well, all there is to tell was that I felt like I was on fire. Or that I was being poked with something. Oh God, am I going crazy!" He yelled to express what he was subjected to was not fun at all. Sleep came to him again as he laid back down on the bed or was it a table he was not sure, but in any case it felt comfortable. Finally he was dreaming of Tommy and himself playing catch just having fun together. Troy longed to love someone; Tommy took a big piece of his heart. For a long time had never felt the need to love to have a relationship or to adopt and have a family in his line of work would never permitted him to. Now it is all going to change he knows that and has accepted it.

CHAPTER ELEVEN

Tommy woke up on the floor he wondered how they had managed to knock him out for he didn't feel it coming. Sitting upright on the floor he put his hand behind his head and rubbed at the knot on the back gently messaging it. He was in total darkness so he could not tell where he was at the moment or could he tell whether or not if he was bleeding from the wound. He did not move from where he laid how long he out was for he had no clue as to what time of day it was. He began to get a hold of his barring he heard a door opening and the lights immediately came on. Squinting from the brightness of the light he closed his eyes for a few minutes and then opened them again. There the Piratain Emperor was standing over him.

"So star child, have you come to your senses about anything that I had said to you earlier?" Tommy looked at him not knowing what he meant about coming to his sense for he had not changed his mind about anything especially about giving him the medallion.

"No, I had not changed my mind about giving you the medallion." He bowed head for it was aching just to look up at the ugliness of the Emperor. "Nor will I ever tell you where it is." Tommy said in a low tone of a voice. He was becoming bored with all their tactic ways of trying to get from him the information the Emperor so greedily requires to complete his mission. He heard the footstep of two guards coming into the room.

"Very well then, maybe we can get what we want by torturing you. Take him to the chamber of games and tortures." Looking up at the two guards who grabbed and dragged him along the floor all the way there. Once inside they had ripped the clothes from his back and chest, tying him down to a cold metal table. They turned away to began to prepare their tools. Tommy was also preparing for the pain that he will have to endure. Closing his eyes he began to remove all pain from his mind as the red hot poker started prodding his abdomen and the sides of his body as they asked him questions over and over. During the whole time Tommy refused to give them anything. After a while the Emperor came in. "That is enough, taking him back to his room. Upon arriving to the room the guards dropped him on the floor and left him alone. Immediately another door opened and two Elurains entered the room and helped him from the floor and to the bed and started attending to his wounds. As he came back into his body the pain of the burns had crippled him to tears.

"Keep hanging in there; do not give up Tommy we are with you."

"Why thank you for the encouragements I do need it." He said. To both of them who looked at him weird.

"My lord, we did not say anything to you."

"Huh," he said as he heard this. "Then who did?" They both shrugged their shoulders for they had no idea what was going on. Tommy opened his mind and he heard shouts of encouragements and support from all of Elura the voices are getting stronger by the minute. He lit up a smile on his face. Now he knew it will soon be time for the ultimate battle against the Piratains. He looked at the two. "All of Elura is calling out to me the two Elurains shared in his joy. In spite of his painful injuries he took pride in the fact that his people were calling out to him.

The Emperor entered his private chambers to be alone so that he could think of what to do with the star child for the torture he had subjected him to had no effect on him. Going to the cabinet he opened it and took out a box, taking it to the table with care he sat it down. Lifting the lid there laid in satin lining were the two other medallions that he possess. Remembering how it felt to win a victory. It was a glorious rush of excitement that flowed through his veins. He longed to feel it again and more, he knew he will never be satisfied with what he has but will always want more. Picking up the medallions from their case he held them up in the air of that the dull light could bounce off them. The medallion has long since lost their gleam to reflective light when the Emperor had ordered the deaths of both the Emperor Abel and Empress Shali of Elura including the star child which at the time Tommy was never to consider being it so he thought. Until now that is, when the Emperor heard this he had sent the search party for Earth to track him down. Making it hard for him to hide, the Piratain Emperors pride himself in that fact that he will soon be Emperor of Elura and his brother was wrong about him not being fit to rule Elura; it was his destiny and his brother and the council took that away from him by banishing him from the planet forever. He knew he will get his revenge someday and now that day has come. The stupid Elurains by rejecting his proposal to start taking other planet for their usage, although it was immediately denied he set to work on a plan to have his brother killed with his brother out of the seat of power then he could resume the throne and order them to except his proposal. Somehow the plan failed for the Elurains already knew of his plans and had interfered by protecting Emperor Abel. He snored while he laughed aloud at the thought up till now he still does not know who had told the council. There was a knock on the door which snapped him back to the present situation.

"What is it?" he yelled angered at who ever dared to invade his privacy.

"My Lord, we have found the other medallion." Not waiting for him to finish, he put the two medallions back into the box and put the box back in its place and went to meet the commander.

"Where did you locate it at?" He felt the rush of power coming over him once more. It was so close he could just taste it.

"On the planet; as far as we know. Now we have another problem there are now two other signals instead of just one. We have yet to find out which one is the medallion to the star child.

"What!" the commander coward backwards so the Emperor could not strike him for failing his mission. "That can't be there is only supposed to one medallion left." He turned away from the commander.

"What do you want me to do my Lord?" Thankfully that he did not strike him. For the commander was ready to please his Emperor with a prize which he has waited so long for.

"Shut up! So I can think for a minute." The Emperor snarled at him. The commander went immediately quite. He waited impatiently for his answer. "Is there any way to bring them here through the transport systems?" The commander thought for a minute.

"Yes, But it will take some time to break through their defense shields which is surround the Central Command Post. The Emperor turned to him with anger in his eyes.

"Well stop wasting time babbling about and just do it!" Anger was rising up in him. "Get going now!" He screamed out in a rage and shoved the commander out of his way. The commander left quickly barking out orders on his way to his station.

The Emperor's rage was getting the best of him, for the other Piratains who were bowing to him he also shoved away from him. The only thing that would calm him down is getting the medallion in his hands. Coming to a stop he found himself in front of the star child's prison room. Nodding his head to the guards as one of them opened the door and they all stepped inside. They entered as the Elurains had left through the side entrance. Seeing the look on the Emperor's face Tommy knew something was not right and was about to find out what it was.

"Well boy." The Emperor said, as he walked farther into the room. "How can there be two more when yours is the last one to the royal throne. I just found out there are three that exist." Tommy just sat there not offering any kind of information. The Emperor crossed over to were he laid prompt up on the bed with pillows behind his head. "You are going to answer me starting now!" Grabbing his arm and dragging Tommy off the bed and onto the floor not caring about hearing his painful grunts. "TALK!" he yelled as he let the rest of his body fall to the floor as he letting go of him. Suddenly the commander ran into the room.

"My Lord, we broke through the shields and are now transporting them." Tommy immediately looked up at the commander to see if he was telling the truth and saw in his mind that he was.

"NO!" Tommy yelled. You leave them alone this is between you and I remember Uncle." The Emperor looked down with surprise that the boy knew. He smiled a knowing grin at him.

"Well, you finally found out who I am." He looked up at the Emperor with a pale face as if he was going to vomit.

"Yes and it disgusts me that I had to call you that. Not anymore you are not part of my family, you're my enemy and I will see to it that you pay for your crimes in one form or another. Just watch and see." At that one of the guards stepped forward and struck Tommy in the face.

"We don't say things like that to the Emperor star child." Bringing a hand up and rubbing the burning sting away as he looked up at the guard.

"I am getting tired of being hit on, as a fair warning you hit me again you will be flying to the other side of this room out of love not hate." The guard looked at him for he did not like it when he said those words. Not caring or wondering about how he was going to manage that trick; so the guard hit him again and the Emperor stood enjoying it. Tommy's head went back turning his eyes on to the guard once more. "I did warn you." His eyes went vacant and the guard went flying to the other side of the room just as he promised that he would do. The guard picks himself off the floor and was in shock at what Tommy had done.

"Bring him!" The Emperor commanded. They were leaving the room the two guards picked him up and dragged him between them. Walking fast so they could keep pace behind the Emperor, so not the miss anything that was to transpire in the next few minutes. Tension was high and the excitement spread throughout the ship as Piratains gathers to witness the victory of their Emperor.

Tommy was thinking very fast to find away to allow the other three to go back to the planet once he had the medallion it would be all over for him as well as for Elura. Tommy could not come to a decision he did not want the humans to be harmed. Even though it was their choosing to be here but fate had brought them together in to this mess and he could only hope things will turn out okay. Reaching the transporting area they waited for the three arrivals readying their weapons pointing to the platform so there would be no escape for their new prisoners.

Troy was sitting up feeling better than he had in years. He buttoned up his shirt over the burnt spot that had formed over his stomach and on his side. Looking up he saw Empress Shali coming towards him.

"Hi." He said as she came into the room.

"Hi yourself you are looking quite well." She smiled.

"Thanks I feel like a millionaire."

"Huh?" She wrinkled her nose; she did not know what a millionaire was.

"It is a person who has lots of money on Earth; they can buy anything they want." He stopped and thought for a second. "Well, almost anything."

"So, what is it that they can not buy?" Troy smiled when she ask the question.

"They can not buy love or true happiness. That has to come from the heart. "If it is the only thing thus far that I have learned since all this began it is to learn to forgive myself and to continue on letting others in here. He pointed to the middle of his chest "to love me and care for me so that I will be able to do the same for others no matter what." He looked away so that she could not tell was he was thinking about. Alan and Faith came in to see how he was doing.

"You okay?" Alan asked.

"I'll live." Getting off the table he stood on his own feet which felt good. They all walk out Troy suddenly felt like he was be lifted up and then the Empress disappeared as did the building that he was in and everything became white all around him. With in seconds a totally different place had appeared Faith and Alan were with him as well. At first it was kind of dark until their eyes had adjusted to the dim lights. Seeing the guards all around them he knew that they were no longer on Elura, but were on the red ship.

"Welcome to my kingdom." The beast said as he stood before them. The Piratain Emperor stepped up to them. Looking at Troy and then down to the medallion. "It was good of you to bring me the medallion, now give it to me?" He spoke to Troy.

"No way am I giving you the medallion!" He spoke loud for all to here. The Emperor was in no mood for this game, so he demanded once again for the medallion. "No!" Was all Troy had to say?

"Then I will take it from you!" The Emperor started forward, Troy tried to get away, but found it virtually impossible for all the guards weapons where on them. When the Emperor had reach out his hand for the medallion it started glowing and blue sparks came from it hitting the Emperors hand. Smoke arose up from the Emperors hand as the smell of burnt flesh started to fill the air as the Emperor let out a painfully scream and immediately backed off holding the injury hand to his chest. Then one of the guards fired his weapon at Troy's shoulder he fell back from the impact. The Emperor had turned to the guard who had fired. "You Fool!" Grabbing the guards weapon The Emperor turned it against the guard and fired at him, as he was vaporized. He turns back to the platform with anger and hate. "Take them away!" He ordered. Troy was picked up by Alan as the guards made way for the off the platform Grabbing his shoulder they were lead away. Passing Tommy he saw tears on the boy's face and wondered if he will ever be free from the Piratains or will he start to fight back. At that moment Troy was not sure of anything. The guard halted him to a stop so he could talk to Tommy telepathically, but he didn't time have to bridge a link between them. Coming up to a room they were shoved inside the door closed and locked behind them. There were Elurains being held in the same room with them. One of them came up to Troy.

"You're wearing the Imperial Medallion." He said out loud for all the Elurains to hear.

"Yes," Troy was trying to sound hopeful so they will continue to hope for the best for their world.

"Where is Tommy being held?" Faith asked. She saw that Elurains didn't know who Tommy was. "The star child," Another Elurain came up to them a girl Faith thought.

"He's being held next door. They wouldn't put him with us for fear that something might happen to him She said. Troy look to the wall were she pointed. Walking over to it he placed his hand on it; closing his eyes he began to concentrate on getting through to Tommy. After a few minutes he began to hear crying in his mind.

"TOMMY WILL YOU PLEASE ANSWER ME?" Troy thought.

"WHO IS THIS?" A trembling voice said.

"IT IS TROY YOU GAVE ME YOUR MEDALLION." He sent a mental picture of him.

"OH MY GOD, THEY HAVE CAUGHT YOU AND A PROMISED THAT THEY WOULD NOT. I HAVE FAILED I AM SORRY IT WAS NOT SUPPOSE TO HAPPEN THIS WAY." The crying was just too much that Troy could not bear to hear.

"HEY, YOU DIDN'T FAIL. IT IS NOT YOU'RE FAULT OKAY. NOW STOP CRYING WE HAVE WORK THAT NEEDS TO BE DONE. I WILL BE HERE TO HELP YOU FROM HERE ON OUT. TOMMY FOR THE FIRST TIME I SAW YOU I KNEW THAT YOU WERE A GREAT KID FOR YOU HAVE CHANGED MY HEART IN SUCH AWAY THAT NOW I AM ABLE TO LOVE INSTEAD OF HATING PEOPLE. I DON'T WANT TO LOOSE YOU. YOU ARE THE KIND OF A SON I ALWAYS WANTED TO HAVE. SINCE THAT IS IMPOSSIBLE I'M WILLING TO GIVE MY LIFE TO SAVE YOURS." Troy broke off for there were tears running down his face. Crouching down on the floor he did not know what to do in this kind of a situation for he has never been a prisoner except inside of himself which he had broken free from now. Finding himself caught off guard and transported without the Central Command Post knowing about it, he hoped that the Elurains will continue to send there thoughts to Tommy for he needs them now more that ever. "TOMMY, YOU STILL THERE KID?"

"YEAH I'M HERE."

"GOOD BECAUSE I WANT YOU TO OPEN UP YOUR MIND TO ELURA FOR THEY ARE THINKING OF YOU." He did Troy began to here a lot of voices coming from Tommy's mind to his. He was glad that the boy wanted to share it with him. He felt his hope being lifted up Troy pulled away once again knowing that Tommy needed to be alone with those voices of his people. He got up wiping his eyes he to needed to be by himself so he could think of a plan that might help all of them.

CHAPTER TWELVE

From the time of the disappearance of the three humans the Central Command Post had been on high alert busy on getting their shields back up and in working order. When they were taken the computer had sent off the emergency alarm. The damage to the shields was only a minor problem that seems to take forever to fix. So that they can work on getting the human back from the grasp of the Piratain Emperor. Empress Shali was wondering how the Piratains managed to break through their shields and transport the three humans in such a short time. Looking outside she watched as the evening approached and the distant lights of the city came on. The sun was now over the horizon and stars twinkle as if all of heavens are watching the out come of the war. For the fate of Elura was now hanging on threads.

Emperor Abel was anxiously pacing the floor waiting for news about the shields. One of the commanders came into the room to inform them that the shields were back online.

"Good now we can get down to business of getting the humans back."

"Sir, I have already tried the transporting systems they are out of range." The Emperor frowned.

"If the Piratains can do it, well then we better find away fast." He said to the commander.

"Yes sir, I will have everyone working on getting them back." He left the room as soon as the Emperor gave him orders. Empress Shali turned to him with sadness in her eyes.

"My love, we can't be like the Piratains you know what will happen if we do." The Emperor smiled at his wife.

"Don't worry it will not come to that I promise, but we do have to try to get the humans back. I am, afraid they will be defenseless against the Piratains.

"Well maybe the little training that you gave them, showing them how to use the medallions, and the emotions that I have planted in them will help as well. Maybe it was time for them to go up there to help our son. Just to remind you in what you use to say and that is to be prepared for the unexpected." She said using his words against him in a loving way for she could never hurt him.

"Okay I'll go easy on our people and except this is destiny taking its course. I'll calm down and not get anxious." He walked to stand beside her. "My only wish right now is to be able to touch you once more. Hold you in my arms as we watch the sun go down together." He looked into her eyes and seeing the same desire.

"That day will come again my love." Lifting up her hand as he did the same their hands went through the others hand. Turning to watch the remaining daylight and darkness settled in.

After a while has past an Imperial Servant had entered the room looking for them. She looked around the room she could not no one so she called on the computer.

"WHAT IS YOUR REQUEST IMPERIAL SERVANT?"

"Where are Emperor Abel and Empress Shali, can you locate them for me?"

"THEY ARE IN THE VIRTUAL REALITY CHAMBERS, AND WISH NOT TO BE DISTURBBED, ONLY IN EMERGENCES."

"Well the Piratain Emperor is on all channels, wanting to speak with the people of Elura."

"I WILL TRANSFERR YOU REQUEST TO THEM."

"Thank you." She left the room.

In the virtual reality chamber the Emperor and Empress were enjoying scenes of different places on Elura the way it use to be until the Piratains decided to make war against them. Some of the scenes are like those of Earth in some way or another except that the colors are a lot brighter on Elura and there weather conditions are always bright and sunny, but in the morning it rains so as to feed the exotic plants, flowers and trees. The wind blows gently afterwards as if to dry them a bit and letting the sun do the rest. It is there dream to restore what had been destroyed by fire. The computer suddenly can in.

"EMPEROR AND EMPRESS I HAVE BEEN INFROMED THE PIRATAIN EMPEROR WISHES TO SPEAK TO THE PEOPLE. HE IS ON ALL CHANNELS. WHAT IS YOUR REQUEST?" The Emperor stopped to think what Troy had said earlier that day.

"Computer, secure all channels except this one." He turns to the Empress. "There is no need for them to hear what he has to say, all he would do is cause them grief and I think that they have had enough of that." The Empress nodded her head in agreement with him.

"AFFRIMATIVE" The scenes went off and there stood the Piratain Emperor.

"What do you want Piratain." Emperor Abel said.

"Ah ha, Abel my brother I have a bargain to strike; do you wish to hear it?" He sounded graceful as if doing them a favor.

"Lets get one thing straight, you are no longer part of my family nor are we interested in any of your bargains or false treaties it is for keeps this time.

"Sorry you are not interested, you leave me on alternative but to eliminate the only son you have, so that makes me Emperor."

"Your threats will not work anymore Piratain; we know that you can not kill him without the medallion in your hand." Empress Shali said.

"Oh, I'll get it alright just as soon as I start having fun with the three humans." The Empress face went pale when she heard that, which meant that he was going to start torturing the humans for the medallion and knowing there is nothing they can do about it, only hoped they will pull through and not give in and giving the medallion over to the Piratain Emperor.

"Bye the way your son knows all about me being your brother, but don't worry he feels the same as you do about me." Emperor Abel looked at him restraining himself from anger.

"Computer, get him out of my sight."

"AFFRIMATIVE" The screen went blank and was replaced back with the scenes of Elura. Looking at them again they found they could no longer enjoy it for the Piratain Emperor had ruined their time together, so they left the virtual reality chamber.

The Piratain Emperor continued to stare at the blank at the screen after he had been cut off from the transmission mode. Now it displayed Elura and its two moons. He enjoyed seeing the Empress turn white when he told her that he was about to have some fun with the three humans. What pleased him most was his brother's anger which he had held back. He knew they had no intentions to tell the star child about him, all he knew they probably had told some story about the tech traders, that is what the Emperor and Empress had told its people. He laughs silently to himself.

"My Lord, we only had one secured channel which was in the virtual reality chamber."

"What a pity, I wonder what the people would say if they knew that their Emperor and Empress Hologram past up a bargain," Shaking in his head in pleasure. "Have the commander prepare the humans to be tortured. I know they can not stand to endure a lot of pain, and then they will give in exchange for their lives I would get the medallion."

"Yes My Lord." He left to do his small task.

The Piratain Emperor walked back to his throne waiting to hear the screams of the humans. He held the box once more in his hands; he had decided that he would keep it next to the throne. For just awhile he would have the last one. Then the war would soon be over without the Elurains suspecting anything is wrong. No sooner had he lifted up the lid of the box he heard the screams the surge of power he was getting had a rush that was much more intense to his dreams of ruling Elura, then when he gets bored with them he would move to Earth. He already decided Earth was worthy to have an Emperor like himself to rule over them. He stopped himself short of his thoughts. He had to get the medallion then he would become unstoppable. Laughing out loud as the screams were coming louder joining in with what he calls wonderful music.

"My Lord, the Elurain Emperor is on a secure channel."

"Put him through." He had never known his brother to call back unless he had come to his sense. Seeing the Emperor's face on screen once again excited him to the bone.

"Brother, I see you have changed your mind about my bargain?" The Piratain Emperor said this; he allowed himself a pleasant smile.

"No not at all! I want to talk to you about surrendering. Give up this senseless war, for it has been going on for far too long." The Piratain Emperor bellowed out a laugh the seemed to ring throughout the ship. He looked back at the screen.

"Have you already forgotten that I have the upper hand in this war, and I can destroy you just like that?" Snapping his thumb and index fingers together a sickening sound of a fierce click ranged out. His lips turned up into a sly smile. "I've had enough talk's dear brother, it is time to act!" With that the screen blank, once more displaying its scene. He turned toward the lieutenant. "Sound the battle alarm." He commanded. "I want an attack on Elura right now!" The lieutenant smiled.

"Well it is about time my lord." He went over to the computer panel and pushes the red button. Immediately the loud drill sounded like that of a siren going off and the ship lights turned blood red. Suddenly Piratains ran hurrying to their stations and to the battle cruisers.

He looked at his wife in desperation.

"It's time for us to call all this to an end. Contact Tommy and tell him it is time to fight and to reclaim what is rightfully his." His wife looked at him with sadness in her eyes hoping Tommy has the courage to fight the powerful Piratain Emperor. Emperor Abel gave her an understanding look and watched her disappear. Suddenly what the Emperor has been dreading has come to past. The high pitch of the computer alarm sounded all through the Central Commander Post quickly Emperor Abel turns to the computer consul, punching a button immediately the commanders pale face appeared. "Report, what is happening?"

"The Piratains are heading this way for an attack sir." The Emperor thought fast and saw it was the prefect time to test out the harmonic frequency weapon that has been installed. He was going to tell the Imperial Council about it, but when he found out Piratains was some how finding out about their next move, he had decided to keep it to himself for the time being. He was glad that he did. He knew the people would not be able to withstand another attack so soon. The harmonic frequency weapon was designed to protect the planet from the Piratains battle cruisers bombardments, but the weapon was never fully test. As he called for the computer he hoped the weapon will work for it is their last resort of this kind of line of defense.

"Initiate the harmonic frequency weapon!" He yelled with anticipation in his voice,

"INITIATION IS COMPLETE." The computer said over the sound of the alarm. A diagram comes up on the large computer screen. The picture of the planet was on the screen and the Piratains battle cruisers were vastly approaching the rim of the planets atmosphere. He lifted up his hand as to give a signal. He yelled.

"Fire the weapon!" Immediately the waves appeared generating its perfectly round circle signals were radiating ripples. Soon one by one the Piratain battle cruisers were disappearing from off the screen until they were on more. Taking no pleasure in killing the Emperor knew it had to be done. "Computer, stop firing the harmonic frequency weapon."

"HARMONIC SYSTEMS ARE OFFLINE." He waited to see if anymore ships were coming. Seeing thus Elura was safe for now; until they find the source of their defenses. The Emperor can only hope that they don't. For the first time he saw hope for Elura. Seeing the commanders face returns to the screen. This time there was a gleam of hope in his eyes.

"The Piratains are retreating for now my lord."

"Excellent." He smiled just keep your eyes on our skies commander and put the defense alarms back online."

Yes Sir," the screen went blank and the light came back to their usual brightness. The silence was immediately broke by the computer.

"EMPEROR ABEL, THE PIRATAIN EMPEREUR IS ON A SECURED CHANNEL, DO YOU WISH TO TALK TO HIM?"

"No, he has had his chance to talk. End transmission." He turned and left the room.

The Piratain Emperor waited for an Elurain to answer, as the screen flashed REQUEST DENIED. He flew in a rage which no Piratain has seen before, his eyes burned red with an evil glow as they felt the ultimate hate flowing out from him. He has crossed over to the point of no return. His fellow Piratains had on idea in what he was capable of; walking over to the commander.

"Send out another fleet of battle cruisers and have them to attack all at once!" The commander did what he had demanded without any questions or remarks for he feared him. The alarm responded to battle mode began again. Immediately the fighters came in and faced the Emperor and he gave them their orders in what to do. After he had finished they took their cue and hurried to the docking bay for another attack on the planet hoping they will succeed this time around. The Piratain Emperor stood in front of the screen waiting as the battle cruisers they had formed a straight line near the planet. They had finished the formation and have waited for the signal.

"Do it now!" He yelled in fury. The battle cruisers went in full speed ahead together as they approached they were immediately destroyed the explosions lit up the screen. The Emperor twirled around to face the commanders again.

"Find out were the source of their defenses is coming from!" The commander's fingers raced along the computer consul.

"My lord, I can not find the source." The commander looked at the Emperor, as he took a weapon off of one of the Piratains side. He lifted it and pointed at the commander.

"You failed." A laser shot out of the weapon hitting the commander in the chest. He disappeared around the corner as he pointed at the lieutenant. "You find out where the source is coming from or you will get the same thing. Shaking his finger at the lieutenant, who took his seat at the consul? He looked his eyes lit up as he had a thought punching a few buttons and in a few seconds he smiled.

"My lord they are using a harmonic frequency weapon that is surrounding the planet."

"Track it to the source and destroy it!"

"Yes my lord, turning back to the computer. "There, it is in the Central Command Post, but they have their shields up so there is no possible way we can destroy it my lord."

"There has got to be away for us to get to them to lower the shields." He went to the consul and stood beside the lieutenant. "There" he pointed for the lieutenant and shook his head. "If we can get them to lower their shields and think that we had decided not to attack again, then we will be already out there already with our battle cruisers in place undetected by their sensors. Then and only then may we have a chance to attack without them knowing what is really happening. He took pride in what he has just thought up. "Good" The Emperor said. "Right now we wait for a while so that they will let their guard down just long enough for us to get through." He walked away to see what is going on with the three humans, and pleased to the fact that they were no longer screaming. He drew closer to the door he noticed that it was opened. Walking inside he saw the humans were not in there. He panicked and it almost slipped his mind that he had sounded the battle alarm, and the ones who were torturing them were battle fighters. Leaving the room he went to were they were being held as prisoners. There were no guards watching the door. He opened it immediately and saw that it was empty. Screaming in a horrendous rage he ran out to get a search party going. "Find them now!" Several of the Piratain left their stations to join in the search.

CHAPTER THIRTEEN

Tommy was still sitting on the floor with his back to the bed and his knees drawn up into his chest. He listened to the millions of voices that were calling out to him with support and encouragements. Feeling better about him self and no longer felt guilty about bringing the three humans from Earth. He could have very well had left the medallion behind, leaving it in a safe place where only him would know where it was, but he decided to follow his mother's instructions. Now feeling helpless for he has no idea what he is supposes to do. With all the powers that he possesses and felt scared not knowing what is going to happen to him in the coming moments. Still listening he heard a voice clearer and louder than the others. In an instant he knew that it was his mothers voice, he looked straight ahead he listened intently.

"Tommy, it is time." Closing his eyes he concentrated.

"It's time for what mother?"

"To reclaim what is rightfully yours. For you to take back the control of Elura and to take it away from your evil Uncle." He did not have to say anything else. Suddenly the battle mode drill ranged for the second time. He heard the foot steps of the two guards take off running leaving him unguarded. Getting up he went up to the door to listen to see if there was any one there. Hearing nothing he looked and saw there was no way to open the door from the inside. Stepping back and looked hard at the door and it had opened on its own. Closing the door behind him he entered the hallway. Being cautious and went to go see what was going on, looking back to see if he had been followed. Tommy hoped he would not be discovered and hurried to the end of the hall. Coming to a halt he could hear the Emperors shouts and commands to attack all at once.

Searching their hateful minds he found the planet was being protected by an unknown weapon. They were not sure of during the first attack. Going back to the hallway taking the same route but this time he had turned the corner. Know that he had to get the prisoners off the ship and back on the planet before the worst of the battle comes. Entering the second hallway there were two Piratains who were outside of the torture room, boasting about how much easier is was to get humans to do what they wanted by inflicting pain on them. Looking up from their small talk they saw Tommy at the end of the hall.

"Hey what are you doing here?" Tommy saw he had taken them by surprise. Not saying any thing he lifted his up above his head as to say that he gave up, and then the familiar sound of thunder the bright light and all was quite it. He looked at them for they where frozen in time. Entering the room he saw them slowly drawing their breath. Shackled and tied to the tables, he looked at each one of them hearing the chains fall off and the straps were undoing themselves. Troy got off the table as he fell to the floor, for the pain he had endured was like it was before when he was on Elura. Slowly he picked himself up. Tommy looked at him with concern.

"Are you okay?" Alan saw him with surprise.

"Yeah, but how did you escape from the two guards?"

"They ran off to do something for the Piratain Emperor." Tommy said without looking at the two guards for he did not know how long they would stay in frozen time. "We have got to hurry to the other prisoners; I do not know how much time we will have left and I want to get them off the ship before anything bad happens to them." Upon leaving the room he gave a smile to Troy even thought he was not looking in his direction. "YOU DID WELL; YOU HUNG IN THERE AND DIDN'T GIVE IN TO THEM." He sent those words to Troy's mind. Who immediately looked towards Tommy and smiled. All of them left the room together in search of the other Elurains. Troy told Tommy the last time they had seem them was in the room that was right next to the one that he was in. "Yeah, I know but getting there was not going to be easy for it is like I maze in here." Troy thought for a moment as they were entering another section of the ship they had never been in since their arrival.

"Tommy, why don't you use your mind and sense out the others as a homing beacon? Maybe we can get there in less time." Tommy immediately stopped.

"Why didn't I think of it before?" He looked at them.

"Well, maybe because I had suggested it." Troy said impatiently as he lean against the wall.

"No, that's not what I meant." He looked down. "Why not transport there." Without anymore comments he stepped a way from them closing his eyes and a portal had appeared putting his hand out to make a grateful gesture all of them were gone and ended up in the room where the Elurains were, like mannequins just waiting to be used. Tommy went around the room and touched each one of them. Sitting down on the chair he felt like he was being drained. Still, he knew that he has to keep on going for time was running out. "Is there away off of the ship"

"Yes," An Elurain girl said. He hadn't seen her since he had been captive.

"How and where?" The girl told him about the three Elurain star gazers that were still sitting in the docking bay near the Piratain battle cruisers. "Then take us there and hurry there is not much time." They all went quickly behind her and in moments they found themselves staring at the three star gazers. Tommy told them to get on board and to start the engines as he went to each ship and did the same thing by touching them they became part of their time period. With last minute instructions to one of the Elurains he looked at the three humans who have decided to stay and help him in his quest. Going back outside of the outer door Tommy waited until they had closed then he pushed the button which opens the docking bay doors. As the ships left, the doors immediately closed by them selves. Running to the observation deck he looked out and seeing the star gazers going as fast as they could when they had entered the atmosphere his hands went up as before and then the blaring of the battle mode came drilling into their ears. They left the room as the four of them covering their ears. Tommy duct into another room that looks like the torture chamber which Faith never wants to see again, but it was someone's living quarters. The lights came on as they entered the room. Sitting Tommy was now feeling worse than he was before his face was getting paler each time he uses his powers for a long amount of time. Faith looked at him with a motherly concern.

"You are not looking well at all Tommy, are you sure you are going to be okay." He nodded his head to her because he was too tired to say anything. Alan looked at them.

"What we got to do now is to devise a plan that will help to make things easier for Tommy's sake." They put their heads together and they began to talk fast to the point that Tommy had lost them in their conversations.

Taking his mind off of what ever they were talking about he turned his thoughts on to the Piratain Emperor who at that very moment was in rage for he could not find them or the Elurain prisoners. Yelling and screaming in anger he commanded that they be found. Seeing there was no one outside of the room they were in now. He tuned into the voices that were getting louder ands now it was getting harder to distinguish who was talking, sometimes it sounded like two or three voices at once. Tommy started to feel tingling come into his body as he continues to listen and his strength was returning. Troy turns to speak to him and saw he was occupied by his thoughts or the thoughts of others. Troy saw the color was returning to his face and was glad the plan he had submitted to the Imperial Council was working out just fine. Snapping him out to it was the worse part.

"Tommy," Troy said as he gently shook him and not talking more than a whisper. Tommy," He shook him a little harder. His eyes had pulled back to the present moment.

"I'm here, I'm here. What is going on?" Troy told him of his plans to get to the other medallions away from the Piratain Emperor, and then he will open a portal so that Faith can go through to Elura and the rest of the fight would be up to him. Tommy stood up and paced the floor as he thought, stopping he looked at them. "It could work, but what if he has them on him?"

"Then we fight to get them back, there will be no easy way out of it." Faith said as Alan finishes the sentence for her.

"The hardest way is the easiest way. That is what my mother use to say when the impossible seemed so hard." Faith rolled her eyes around in her head.

"Men you can't bare with them and you can't live without them. Now that is impossible." Alan laughed out of good nature, but being cautious about his voice. Tommy's head went up in alarm as he felt someone coming their way.

"Quick hide there is someone coming?" The door opened as they did not have time for that. Three Piratains stood at the door with their weapons drawn and pointed out at them. Still they looked around and seeing nothing they went on to the next room. This raised questions in all of them as they looked at Tommy.

"Did you do that?" Faith said as she got up from the floor.

"I don't know what the heck I did, all I did was wished that they would not see us here." Shrugging his shoulders he himself had no idea how it had happened. He placed his ear to the door so to hear if the three Piratains were gone. Opening it Tommy stuck out his head seeing nothing he wave his hand onward to the others signaling to them to come for the cost was clear. They slowly came up to the throne room the shouts and unpleasant talks of what the Piratain Emperor was saying of what he would do to them when they were found. Silence fell as the lieutenant came in.

"My lord, the three stare gazers are missing from the docking bay and it is my guess they have left the ship without anyone noticing it while we were attacking the planet." The Piratain Emperor was screaming out threats which were not carried out. Just saying them made him feel better for he was lost and did not know what to do next. So he ordered everyone to clear the throne room so he could have a moments worth of peace so he could think up a strategy to fight back with. Waiting for the room to clear and Tommy heard him settling down on the throne with a loud sigh. Stooping so that he would not be noticed he saw the Emperor taking something in his hand and threw it, as it smashed up again the wall.

"It isn't over until I say it's over star child." He yelled it so the echoes of his own voice sliced the air with a coldness which had radiated from the very core of his hatred for Tommy and for the planet of Elura. Getting up he went to the place in which he hid the medallions. He smacked his hands together with glee and a laugh of pleasure when he saw that he still holds the two pieces. "At least he forgot about taking the medallions with him. Since I can not have his then I still can take the one that I have. After all I am still part of the family whether they like it or not." Tommy saw him lifting up the inner case and he brought out yet another medallion even the Elurain Emperor and Empress had probably long since forgotten about the medallion the Piratain Emperor holds. Taking all three of them he went to the other side of the room where all of them could see what he was doing. Touching a panel the wall slid down revealing a device of some kind. Placing each of them inside the device he gave the computer the latitude and longitude.

"WHAT IS YOUR PRIMARY TARGET?"

"Target the sun."

"TARGET IS LOCKED AND READY FOR YOUR COMMAND."

"Good! Now lets see if what the planet has to say for them selves when I tell them that the whole solar system is about to meet its end! Open a channel to the Central Command Post; if they refuse tell them it is a matter of life and death for all who live within this solar system. That should get there attention. After all I get to pull the switch on them." He shouted for the lieutenant to return to the room.

"Yes my lord." Turning around to face the Piratain Emperor for he had a dark gleam in his eyes.

"Prepare all engines to move on to the next solar system." The computer had cut him off.

"THE ELURAIN EMPEROR WILL SPEAK WITH YOU NOW ON A SECURE CHANNEL ONLY."

"That will have to do; I guess everything I say for now on would probably be on a secure channel." Instructing the lieutenant on what he wants for him to do. Hesitating a little for the lieutenant wondered if the Emperor was not only loosing control, but loosing his mind as well. In any case he did not wish to be the Emperor's next victim. So he quickly left to do as he was told. After the lieutenant left Tommy told the others to wait there, he began to inch his way little by little being careful so the Piratain Emperor would not see him. He saw his fathers face on the screen the Piratain Emperor making him surrender or he would have no choice but to destroy them all. When Tommy came in to view hearing the shakiness in his voice he did realize his father could see him. He shook his head in telling his father to pretend that he was not there, and to keep him talking as long as he could. He hurried soundly the rest of the way towards the device the medallions sitting neatly side by side. Tommy looked at it for he had no idea how to take them out without being noticed he was hoping the computer did not have an alarm on it. Putting his hands on the device he closed his eyes for a second, quickly he opened them just as the medallions were falling to the floor. Suddenly he focused on them as they where suspended in midair. Grabbing each one of them he turns to go back to where the others were when the Piratain Emperors rage came to a halt everything that was happening.

"I am tired of playing your squeamish little talk games Elurain Brother it is now time to destroy you and all your planet holds dear to them! Computer fire when ready!" Seeing the Elurain Emperors mouth dropped as to say this can't be the way it was supposed to go.

"UNABLE TO FIRE THE WEAPON IS WITHOUT THE REQUIRED PIECES."

"What!" Turning around he saw Tommy crouching low. "You, how could it be, I thought you left with the rest of the escapees!" Now being caught in the act he stood to his full height.

"You thought wrong, don't think that I will allow you to destroy the planet not to mention the whole solar system where there is life." Tommy looked him dead in the eyes. "Your sadly mistaken, anyway don't belong to you." He held up the medallions so the Piratain Emperor could see they are now in his possession of them. Stunned the Piratain Emperor fell backwards in denial to the fact the stare child has out smart him in his plan to conquer his supposed to be destiny. Regaining his composure he rushed at Tommy to take the medallions back from him by force. Tommy threw them to the others who now stood ready for action in any form in which it came. Faith and Alan had caught them instantly a portal had appeared. Just as a guard came in to the room to see what was going on. The Piratain Emperor pointed to Faith and Alan, screaming at the guard to get them. As he started running towards Faith, Alan and Tommy saw two other guards.

"Go now!" He shouted to them. In an instant both of them ran towards the portal and dove in just as the guard was at there heel. The guard tried to go in after them, but the portal quickly disappeared and the guard landed flat on his stomach grunting in pain.

"You fool you will pay for not getting them!" The Emperor raced at Tommy and he had his hands around the boys' throat. Tommy gasps for air as he tried to pry the Emperor's hand away from his throat. Finding it impossible he thought of what he was taught; now instead of fighting he held out his arms to welcome death. Suddenly there was a burst of white light which came from the center of his chest and radiated outwards then became a force which threw the Emperor across to the other side of the throne room. He hits the wall not caring about any thing but killing the star child.

During this time Troy was about ready to help Tommy when he was grabbed from behind and slammed up against the wall. Feeling like he was going to pass out from the blow, he continued to tell himself he has to be there for Tommy's sake and on the other side of his mind was telling him not to worry the kid has it all under control. Seeing the burst of light surrounding the boy gave him the strength to endure all that he possibly could. Coming back to his senses Troy knew he was going to need all of the strength he could muster up to fight not only his but Tommy's survival. Thinking of only his love for the boy all of a sudden he grabbed the Piratain by the front of his uniform and realizing with astonishment he was holding the Piratain off the floor and was looking at him.

"Now it is my turn." Throwing the guard away form him as if he was a bag of garbage he was throwing away in to a bin. The Piratain guard let out a scream as he went through the air. Looking around to the other guard who was on his feet and almost made it to the door to get more help. The guard felt a hand on his neck as Troy was dragging him back into the room and sending him on a collusion course with the other guard. As they hit each other, he heard the grunts of pain they were enduring and actually saw fear come into their eyes for neither one of them got up to help the Emperor.

CHAPTER FOURTEEN

Emperor Abel stood at the screen watching as the events were beginning to unfold right before his eyes until the screen went blank as the Piratain Emperor was being slammed into the wall beside the screen on the ship. Looking away from it the Emperor was wondering if Tommy and the others would survive the battle they had just begun. Not allowing him self to dwell on the worst of things, but that of the good. Turning from the screen he went towards the door as one of his commanders almost ran right through him.

"Sorry my lord, I did not realize you were coming out." He said as he abruptly stopped then took a step backwards he nearly forgot the Emperor was a hologram that he could not be hurt.

"That is okay, no harm done. So what is this running all about?" He looked at the commander hoping it is good news for he didn't know how much of this war he could endure.

"Two of the humans are back. With three medallions and I was told by the Empress to come and get you. Both of the humans are being treated for they were hurt as they came through a portal the star child had created." The commander continued to talk as the Emperor disappeared right in front of him. "I'll never get use to the things they are able to do with the computers help of course." He turned back and went back to were he came. Emperor Abel appeared inside the infirmary seeing the blood on Alan's shirt and saw the cut just above the eyebrow on his left side.

"Are you okay?" He said to Alan while looking over to where Faith was sitting up.

"Yeah, we just had a bumpy ride on the way back down here." Faith injected. Still feeling the dizzy spells starting up again she had been tumbling over and over inside the portal and when they came out, it felt to her that they were being thrown by an unknown force when all the while it was the force of the wind that was caught inside with them. Digging inside of her pocket of her frock she had produced one of the two remaining medallions and she was sure that Alan had the other two. Handing it over to the Emperor he smiled for it was the one that was made for him before his birth. Faith realized that the Emperor could not take it because of the form he was in, so she gave it to the Elurain nurse who went out after she got the other two from Alan. Empress Shali had appeared as well to look in on them. Smiling at them she thanked them for risking their lives to bring them back to its rightful place. She turns to the Emperor.

"Now how much of the beginning of the battle did you see?" He smiled at her and assured her things are going to be just fine form here on out.

"Oh, I saw the Piratain Emperor being thrown up against the wall before the screen went out."

"Where is Troy?" She said to Alan.

"He's still on the ship helping Tommy. I guess he felt he wanted to stick around to kick some butts." Empress Shali frown at him, not because of the word he had chosen to speak, but the fact Troy had choose not to come back with the other two. Alan looked at her. "Why what is wrong?"

"Nothing just concerned that is all." She then looked at her husband and walked to a corner of the room as he followed her.

"What is going on with you?" He said with concern in his voice.

"He should have returned with them. He's going to get himself killed if he does not know how to use the medallion properly." She folded her arms around her chest.

"Don't worry your self my dear, because in my heart I know he has learned how. All we can do wait to see." He turned from her so that Faith and Alan would not think something was terribly wrong. Alan sat up after the nurse had put something on the cut which is on longer there, and feeling as if he could go back to the ship for round two. Faith on the other hand told him she has had enough to last her a lifetime. Empress Shali came forward.

"I'm afraid letting you go back Alan is out of the question. We can't seem to get our transporters to work correctly. She said as a matter of fact. With his shoulder he shrugged the idea off; thankful he didn't have to go back. His heart told him he could not just leave one of his own on a ship full of evil Piratains to fight let alongside a very remarkable boy who seems to be turning into a man before his very eyes. Still he wonders if they will make it out okay. Knowing it was what was on every ones mind. Faith got up from the table and went to Alan's side slipping her hand into his. She knew the love she has for him had only just begun and that there would be no other. Alan looked up from his deep thoughts and finally laid them to rest when he looked into Faith's eyes and saw the love that she had for him.

Sensing that they needed to be alone the Emperor and Empress had asked for everyone to leave the infirmary so they can have their moments of peace together. They both vanished from the room both Faith and Alan were thankful to them for giving them time to each other which since they had met on the long journey was the first time since that night at Alan's apartment.

Both Emperor Abel and Empress Shali had entered the main area where their people were going everywhere as the information they had been collecting began to pile up. The same commander came to them with news about the weapon on the Piratain ship was pointed out in the direction of the sun was most likely to be the weapon that would have destroyed our planet it was the only so far weapon the Piratain Emperor need the medallion pieces to help power the weapon. Now that he does not have the medallions he could not use it for all the money it was worth to build it. The computer alarm was no longer silent when they have felt that they were in danger of an attack and made ready the harmonic frequency weapon to rid their enemies. With it to protect was their only chance for survival. The alarm was cut off as an Elurain cam in hurrying to where the Emperor and Empress were standing.

"Sir, we have identified three ship and they are ours. Our people have escaped the red ship and are coming in for a landing."

"Good, have a team ready to asset them. Also get the Imperial Council there is something that needs to be gotten out in to the open." The Elurain bow his head and then left to do the Emperors bidding. As he was leaving the nurse who was with them in the infirmary and had the three medallions came to them.

"My Lord, I have had the medallions checked to see if they are real the real ones and we have discovered the third one." The Emperor had cutting her off.

"My dear, I know who the other medallion belongs to it is for that reason I have called a meeting with the Imperial Council. You are welcome to attend the meeting if you wish. All will be explained in due time." The Emperor looked gravely tired, and knew the Imperial Council would not improve in what actions he had taken in lying to them about his brother, for at the time they wouldn't understand what the high council at the time requested banishing his brother off the planet for his wrong doing of plotting to kill him, and that the people didn't need to know the truth. Empress Shali looked at him with love in her eyes.

"What ever happens I will be right there by your side always. He smiled.

"You know the worst thing they can do are disconnecting the hologram projection to terminate me."

"They can do the same to me, because I will not continue with out you beside me." She assured him that he would not be standing alone in the sentencing. "We did cause this war in away, but lying to them is considered wrong in their eyes no matter the reason. I just hope that they will understand our actions that we took and will be merciful on our behalf." looking to her husband and see the comfort setting in., then talks were switched to concerns for Troy Beckman and Tommy who are still on the red ship. The commander came in.

"The Imperial Council is ready and waiting my lord." Both the Emperor and Empress fell in behind the commander as they followed him into the meeting place.

Faith and Alan came out of the infirmary hand in hand for they have been talking about what they were going to do when this whole thing is over with. They have come to an agreement that if the Emperor and Empress would allow them to stay on Elura and live. They both felt that it isn't the right time to say anything about it yet, so they would wait and find out afterwards. Entering the main section they saw other Elurains were taking care of the escapees from the ship. Alan had thought that they would have arrived before they left by the portal that Tommy had created. They didn't know that time slows down on the outside of the portal and that is why they were just getting there. Both Alan and Faith had quick set in motion and helping them and giving them moral support when they needed it, Thankful that they were given something to do, instead of sitting of their gluteus maximus and pacing back and forth waiting for news good or bad. As a little boy came in crying for his mother, Faith went to him and asked him what she looked like. After a while she managed to find her and the little boy ran into her arms for only the comfort of his mothers touch was the only thing that would smooth away the child's fears. She stood there Faith wondered if she would ever have a child of her own, to love and care for just as her parents had done for her so many years ago. Until that fateful night when the police had came to her door while she was asleep in her bed. She was just starting in her early teens. The sitter came into the room telling her that her parents that she was needed downstairs. Putting on her robe and thinking that her parents had a surprise for her. They had often had her get up when they got home just to give her a gift and to remind her that they would always love her. Faith was the only child that they could have and her parents wanted her to know by spoiling her in a very special way. Taking the stairs two at a time she was met by two uniformed police officers. Not sure what to think of it, for she knew her parents would never play a trick on her. Looking from one man to the other neither of them could manage to meet her eyes. Instead they would only look down as they told her about the drunk driver who had collided head on into her parent's car. As they were heading to the hospital her farther had died on the way and her mother was fighting to stay alive in the I.C.U. Faith told her self that it was a bad dream and that she would wake up any minute now, finding herself still inside of the living nightmare she allowed the officers to take her by the arms gently guiding her to the car. Seeing her mother in the bed with tubes and needles stuck in her arms reminded her of the Barbie doll she had used to play doctors with. Leaving the room for a minute a man had grabbed her and slurring out load that he did not see them coming, he smelled of liquor on his breath. He pleaded with her to forgive him. It was at that time she would never trust a man with her life and that she would never come to love one. Her mother had survived but left scars on her as a reminder of that night. Her mother had never gotten over the death of her father which forces Faith to take care of her mother until she died when Faith was eighteen years of age. Ever since then she had always been afraid for her own life. Being careful about her driving and she never allowed herself any time to make friends while she was in college and all the way through her career she had been alone. Until now being given back the courage to do things she would never do as far as putting her life in danger and the love that she now has for Alan Tate and swore to her self that she would never loose it again. Feeling a hand on her shoulder brought her back into the present. Looking over to see it was Alan. Grabbing his hand on her shoulder and giving it a squeeze.

"You know, for the first time in my life I am not afraid anymore, and allowing me to love and to put myself in danger to help another person I love and care about. Does that sound so selfish for me to do?" She looked at him and waited for his reply.

"No, it just means that you have found something that you were not looking for and or trying your hardest not to have, because of all that you been through. You thought it was something that was not met to be. I'm sure glad that you decided to take a chance on it." Alan pulled her to him and continued to watch the mother and the little boy who was now smiling as if nothing had happened. Leaving them to their own happiness both of the continued to stay busy until there was nothing left to do, but to sit and rest them selves so they can be ready for what ever comes next. As they continued to watch the people, they did not realize the Emperor and Empress was standing next to them until they had looked up.

"Hi," Alan said. "So, what is going on mow?" He was not trying to be comical.

"Well, we have just finished the meeting with the Imperial Council, telling them what the Piratains really are and how this war came about and why had to kept it a secret for a long time. Not telling them the reason we did what we did. But we told them why the reason they had lied about not telling the truth at this time, well, they were still shocked in learning the truth." The Emperor brought his head down. "I feel as if I have failed my people in some way, while trying not to hurt them in any way. You know, like being there for them and yet you are not I suppose." Seeing him upset Faith knew the feeling of helplessness for she had been friends with it for a long time.

"Don't let it get you down, but instead look on the bright side of things. You got the truth out and it is no longer on your conscious for the rest of your life." Forgetting the they are holograms, but to Faith they seem just like any other being, for she did not consider them dead, but alive. Though she never seem a dead person walking around trying to save his world or what is left of it. The Emperor looked up at Faith he saw that she didn't consider them to just be there as a hologram but had made him feel that much more alive than he use to feel. For all the time she just felt like a thing to get the rules and regulation from and not a person.

"Thanks, I needed that." Looking at his wife humans are such wonderful people aren't they?"

"Yes I am just please to have the few here with us." She smiled at both of them. An Elurain approached them, bowing before the Emperor and Empress.

"They are ready for both of you to hear their decision on your case. Please follow me."

"Well, both of us are with you inspirit and in mind." Faith said as they walked away

"Good luck!" Alan yelled after them. He hoped the best for the two. As they walked behind the Elurain, find that he did not offer any kind of hint on to what the Imperial Council had decided. So he had to be patient and wait and see for them self. Entering the chamber all talks had immediately stopped when they had walked in and took their seat. As their anticipation started to mount they could no longer take the silence. Before the Emperor could speak the Imperial Council Member stood.

"The Imperial Council has decided that you are not at fault for what you both did and acted only for the interest of your people, since you willing came forward on your own will it is only fitting that the Imperial Council did the same." Both the Emperor and Empress looked at each other questionably. "For when we had to decide to put you and the Empress on a ship with your son bounded for Earth, we couldn't let you go so what we did is put you both in frozen stasis and had made doubles of you and the holograms to where your subconscious mind will be free to wonder. We had to use your medallions to do all this and by the time the Piratain Emperor had them there was no way to bring you out of the frozen stasis that is until today. We sincerely hope that you will forgive us for our part in keeping secrets. Both the Emperor and Empress had their mouths open in the shock of what they had just heard. The Emperor stood.

"Imperial Council if this is indeed all true then my wife and I owe you all a debt of gratitude, Although that we kept secrets from one another is not good, we did it to preserve our race and to save this planet Both side did it for the greater good of things, but we almost lost sight of each others pain. So just as you see no fault in us, we see no fault in you, but from this day forward we need to be honest with one other, because if we are not then we stand divided and trust will going out the door. Is this a deal the Imperial Council can keep?" They talked among themselves and quickly came back to order.

"The Imperial Council agrees no more secrets." They all stood and clapped their hand on this great day and had been decided not to bring the Emperor and the Empress out of frozen stasis yet until after the war is over. It brought great relief to know that they are not dead but frozen. And know that soon they will be holding their son and each other again soon. Standing up the Emperor went to the Window and looked out to the darken skies of Elura for a new day will soon be dawning. It had been a long night even for Faith and Alan who were sleeping side by side while sitting up in a chair. The Empress did not want to bother them for they needed their rest, as do all of their people do for they have been working around the clock day and night taking shift so that the planet would not go unprotect. Even with the computer's help it seems to be a lot of works for there were times when the engineer would have to stay up long hours trying to repair what had been damaged. All of them are waiting for the time when this would be nothing but a memory. Life would be so much easier to live and comfortable.

These are the days the Empress sees. Where they are taking care of each other and teaching their young the ways of life. Where there is no fear of living in hiding from their enemies. For there will be peace thorough out the world. Rejoicing on the day of victory of freedom one and for all times to come. The beauty of there planet will once more grow and blossom as far as the eye can see. There will be no more reminder of war. She smiled to her self for the vision of the future to come to Elura. She has hoped and knows that it will come true. It is their destiny no evil of any kind can take it a way from them no matter what. As the suns first rays hit the ground Empress Shali left to do her duties as Emperors wife. To take care of its people no matter what time it is. Now that everything was slowly becoming clearer to her, she will summon the people together to witness the final destruction of the evil that has enslaved them all. She had no doubt in her mind that her son will destroy the Piratain Emperor and its ship and come home alive.

CHAPTER FIFTEEN

The Piratain Emperor got up as he saw the two guards still on the floor, in a great rage he went to them and started to kick them for their stupidity. After a while he turned and faced the star child again, his anger had no boundaries his eyes grew a deep blood red and his body seems to be getting bigger. The two Piratain guards screamed out in pain as their bodies began to convulse and start changing before Troy's very eyes. After a while they laid there not moving. From the brightness that Tommy's body was putting out Troy had a hard time seeing what was happening to them, so he went a little closer and saw in astonishment that they some how reverted back into their former selves as Elurains which is their true nature. Immediately he went to help them up, they looked at Troy confused and unaware of their surroundings. Standing Troy grabbed both of them by the arms and rushed them out of there, grateful for the fact that the Emperor was on longer interested in them. He looked back once more before leaving the room and saw in terror the Piratain Emperor was no longer recognizable. Not wasting any more time he went to the control area as he heard the screams coming from all over the ship. He instructed the two to go and help the others who are reverting back to their natural state. Troy realized that the Piratain Emperor was drawing all of the anger and ambitions out of them. Thinking fast he knew that there had to be a way to get them all off the ship.

"Computer, where are the transporters?" He said for he had no idea what else to do. He knew nothing about the ship or its functions.

"TRANSPORTERS ARE ON THE LOWER LEVEL, BUT ARE NOT TO BE USED MANUAL REPAIR NEEDS TO BE DONE." Troy hit the consul in determination to get off of the ship, and then he thought of the docking bay.

"Are there still ships docked?"

"AFFIRMATIVE" He quickly asks for a channel to be opened to the planet. "NEED MORE REPAIR TIME?"

"How much more time to need?"

"FOUR MINUTES UNTIL REPAIRS IS COMPLETE." He told the Elurains to start for the docking bay, but not the lift off until they heard from him. The two Elurains nodded their heads to acknowledge Troy's request. They started walking the hallway that leads to the docking bay and on the way they pick the rest of the Elurains.

"Computer, are there anymore Piratains on board?" Troy waited for an answer.

"There is only one Piratain on board."

"That is good." All the Piratains other than the Emperor had reverted to their natural state as an Elurain. He watch as the last one was out of the control room. Now with out the confusion that was coming from them Troy was able to think more clearly. The computer came back on voice mode.

"REPAIRS COPMPLETE, REQUEST FOR AN OPEN CHANNEL?"

"Yes, tell the Elurain Emperor that Troy Beckman needs to talk to him."

"AFFRIMATIVE" He waited sum more. "REQUEST IS COPMPLETED." The screen came alive with static interference and then a clear picture of the Emperor appeared.

"Emperor, I am going to be sending the rest of the Elurains to you, they will be using the Piratain battle ships, so do not be alarm when they appear on you sensors."

"Has all the Piratains reverted to their former selves' again?"

"Yes, we don't have much time, so be prepared." The screen went blank. "What happened?"

"MANUAL REPAIRS NEEDED ON CHANNELS."

"Forget the manual repairs the message had gotten across." Troy raced to the computer consul. Punching in buttons hard he turned around in frustrations, "Computer prepare for the ships to leave the docking bay."

"AFFRIMATIVE, YOUR REQUEST IS UNDER WAY." Troy gave the go head to left off. As the docking bay door open he made sure that they were cleared and would be okay from that point on. Turning around he then started back to the throne room to help Tommy hoping that he is still okay when he suddenly stopped and smacked the side of his face in realization came in.

"Computer, Are there anymore Elurains on board this ship?"

"THERE ARE FOURTY-FIVE ELURAINS ON BOARD AND FIVE HUMANS, NOT INCLUDING THE STAR CHILD AND THE PIRATAIN EMPEROR NOR TROY BECKMAN." When he heard this the ships were already cleared from the docking bay.

"Show me where they are?" The computer displayed a map that appeared on the wall above the consul. Troy continued to work franticly on the consul. "Is there anyway to transport them in to the throne room?"

"AFFRIMATIVE, THE EMERGENCY TRANSPORT SYSTEMS ON THE SHIP ONLY IS WORKING." Troy shook his head.

"Why didn't you tell me this before I started running around here like a mad man?"

"YOU DID NOT ASK." Troy shrugged it off. "SHALL I BEGIN TRANPORTTING?"

"No, not until I get to the throne room." "Is there another way off this ship now?" He knew that answer to that, but had to be sure.

"NEGETIVE, ALL BATTLE SHIPS HAD LEFT AT YOUR REQUEST AND ALL TRANSPORTERS ARE OUT EXCEPT FOR THE EMERGENCY TRANSPORTER ON SHIP ARE DOWN." As he entered the throne room the rest of the remaining hostages were arriving Troy looked and recognized an F.B.I agent that he used to work with. A black hair tough looking guy came running towards Troy.

"Agent Beckman, this is a surprise to see you?" Looking him in the eyes which seem to say am I going crazy or is this dream. Troy assured him that this is very real.

"Agent Hansen, how do you feel? The man scratched his head and gave Troy a confusing look. "I know that this is hard or too much to take in, but if we are ever going to get out of here I am going to need your help in keeping these people under control so I can think about another way out of here. Troy pointed to the group of Elurains out to him to see. Not having to say nothing else. Agent Hansen understood and set him self to work.

"TRANSPORT IS COMPLETE." WHAT IS YOUR REQUEST NOW SIR?" Troy turned to a consul near where Tommy and the Piratain Emperor were still at it.

"Computer, are you capable in answering any question no matter how weird they seem to you?"

"YES, WHAT IS YOUR REQUEST?"

"If you were in a situation where there is no way out and you have a medallion, what would you do?" Touching the cool surface, for he almost forgot that he had it.

"UNABLE TO ANSWER QUESTION, MEMORY BANKS CAN NOT PROCESS." Suddenly there was a rumble that shook the ship.

"What is happening?" he asked the computer.

"THE SHIP IS ON OVERLOAD, EVACUATE SHIP, EVACUATE SHIP." Troy swore under his breath. "YOU HAVE TWENTY MINUTES TO EVACUATE SHIP." Closing his eyes he concentrated on getting in Tommy's mind. Sensing the evil coming from the room he began to probe harder and suddenly he fell backwards for accidently entered the Piratain Emperor's mind. He felt all that anger and hostility which he possessed. He caught himself on the corner of the consul. He relaxed and tried it again.

"Tommy, your people and mine are going to die if we do not get them off the ship. Tell me what to do?" This time he felt Tommy's mind and hoped that he had gotten through and that the Emperor was to busy to notice that he had entered his mind by mistake. Opening his eyes he waited for a reply.

"Use the medallion to create a portal; you have to use all that is inside of you!" Troy grabbed his head for the intensity of Tommy's voice was louder than he was expecting. Going down on one knee he thought that his brain would explode any minute. After the message had finished Troy took his hands away slowly not sure what will happen. He rested for a few seconds he looked up and saw Agent Hansen running towards him in concern.

"You okay?" He bent down to help Troy to his feet. Nodding his head for he did not have the voice to say anything. Running his nose on his sleeves of his shirt he noticed that he had a nose bleed from the impact of Tommy's voice in his head.

"FIFTEEN MINUTES TO EVACUATE THE SHIP!" Even the computers voice was getting louder in its warnings.

"Agent Hansen I will need you to move the people to the other side of the throne room, just don't get close to the altercation that is brewing."

"For what, are we all going to die?" He said frantically as he started to panic as another rumble shook them off their feet. Both of them herd the screams of the Elurains. The remaining humans came towards Troy and Agent Hansen to find out what was going on. Agent Hansen saw them coming and he waved them back with the others. Seeing them going back he turned to Troy for answer.

"I will need the room to create a portal. It is the only way out." For the time he and Hansen were working together. The man had always wanted the precise detail before doing what he was told and Troy hoped that he wouldn't waste any more time. Hansen got up and helps Troy up, and then he went to go move the others to the side of the room. Troy was grateful to him for not doubting. Bringing the medallion out of his shirt he took it in between his thumbs and index fingers. Lifting it off from around his neck and held it high above his head. Concentrating, he envisioned a portal like the one he had seen Tommy make. Pouring out his feeling, he could feel the air in front of him begin to stir as the force became stronger. He did not dare to open his eyes, and then brightness hits his eyes lids. "Go now!" He yelled. He didn't know how long he can keep it open. Sensing that everyone was now inside the portal he opened his eyes and saw not only one but three portals opened up at the same time. Looking about the room seeing that it is empty besides himself the Tommy as well as the Piratain Emperor. Feeling exhausted he clasped to the floor for it took just about every fiber of his being to create the portals. He lies on the floor for a few minutes.

"EVACUATION COUNTDOWN TERMINATED, ALL SYSTEMS ARE DOWN." Troy looked up wondering how the countdown was terminated.

"Computer why was the evacuation countdown was terminated?"

"SHIP MAINPIPELINES HAVE BEEN REPAIRED. THERE IS NO IMMDEIATE DANGER."

"Okay" was all Troy could say. He pulled himself up by using the computer consul. Not realizing that the Piratain Emperor was in back of him until the hairs on the back of his neck stood up. He turned around to see who it was. He was grabbed by the shirt and thrown half way across the room. Hitting the floor again and the medallion that he held in his hands hit the floor with a clang and rolled the rest of the way to the wall which was a couple of feet from Troy. The Piratain Emperor went over and picked it up with some sort of staff. Troy watched the medallion hanging on the stick he looked at the Emperor who seems to be smiling he couldn't tell for his features were distorted and his eyes still glowed with fury.

"With the star child dead, this medallion will not help you." He said in a deep voice.

"You're lying!" Troy said determined and know that Tommy was indeed still alive, he was sure of it. The Emperor came back to him.

"Oh am I" Giving Troy a sickly smile, grabbing him by the collar he dragged Troy as if he was a blanket. He squirmed trying to get away from the beast as he was tossed the rest of the way he landed near Tommy as he felt dizzy and sick he didn't want to see if the Emperor was telling the truth. He dare not let go of the hope and the love he has for Tommy no matter what happens next. "See for yourself human." Watching Troy regain his senses lying on his stomach lifting his head he looking at the Emperor standing pointing with a long talon finger Troy had slowly followed with his eyes as it came upon Tommy's body laying on his back with blood coming from his mouth, from experience he knew there was internal bleed. Troy's anger mounted and was about to surface once again, holding it back with all that her had and was determined not to become that man ever again.

"No!" He cried in desperation sliding him self over to where Tommy laid lifting his head gently cradling it in his lap wiping the blood from the corner of his mouth with his shirt.

"How touching!" The Emperor said with a snicker in his voice. Troy's head shot up with tears in his eyes and seeing the Emperor as a monster for the first time with no other feeling but hate. With a new found strength putting Tommy's head back down to the floor and stood up, stepping away from the body and putting some distance way between him and the evil Emperor.

"Now, I will finish what he started." He said. The Emperor howled in laughter.

"You, he pointed at Troy. Oh, I'm so scared!" As the Emperor mimicked what a little child would usually say when they have the upper hand. He shook his body and hands as if he was trembling in fear. Then another howl of laughter escapes the Emperor's mouth as he put his hands to his hips assuming that is what they are he couldn't really tell. For the laughter now was uncontrollable. Without thinking Troy stretched out a hand and the medallion flew into it before the Emperor could regain his composure. Immediately the Emperor stopped laughing for Troy had caught him by surprise. "You are beginning to annoy me human!" Troy then brought the medallion above his head. "Don't do that!" The Emperor yelled. He saw a flicker of fear surfacing in the eyes of the Emperor as he gripped the staff he held tightly in his big hands looking as if it might snap in two under its pressure. The Emperor saw the gleam in Troy's eyes and knew that he was not going to back down any more.

"Why does it scare you?" he said as he closed his eyes and allowed the love to flow threw him he felt the warmth of the medallion enter his hands and spread all over him as if he were standing in the sun on a nice warm day. The Emperor saw the medallion grow bright and suddenly a bright beam hit him square in the chest knocking him off his feet and hurled across the room. He hit the wall with a painful thump. "Let see how you like being thrown around for once." Troy said. The medallion continued to grow with intense brightness now outlining Troy's body like a protective shield.

"No!" The Emperor said with a lingering shout. He became frustrated as he got up from the floor. Thinking of what his next move might be no sooner had he thought it he was suspended in mid air and the shot forward head first into a computer consul, sparks few from the impact. The Emperor squint his eyes in pain as he fell. He saw that he still held the staff looking at Troy he threw the staff towards the medallion knocking it from his hands. The brightness that was forming and the surge of power that ran through him was now gone. "Now you will pay!" With a grin the Piratain Emperor's eyes glow red with hate for Troy. He opened his eyes just as the Emperor grabbed him and slamming him into a wall, not letting go he was slammed up against the wall a second time was about ready to slip into a daze when the Emperor dropped him on the floor kicking him in the ribs. "Humans always take it the hard way." He said as he amused himself with watching Troy squander in pain. Every time he tried to get up the Emperor kicks him back down. Troy was feeling the rush of pain as the Emperor continued to kick him not wanting to give the Emperor the satisfaction of his evil deeds. He kept silent refusing to give in for that will be too much to bear and that will please the Emperor greatly. Giving Troy one final and swift kick into the ribs, for the enjoyment he felt was gone and found Troy less entertaining. Looking about searching for the staff that he had thrown, upon finding it he retrieved it. Not allowing Troy any time to react in his rebellion and try to attack him again with the medallion. Locating the circular object he looked down upon it and felt his anger arising again taking the staff he knocked the medallion under the computer consul as if he had just scored a goal hearing a soft thud indicating that it is beyond Troy's reach. Standing there he watched Troy coming back to his senses and that his strength was returning. Meeting

Troy's gaze, the Emperor's formless lips curled up at the corner of his mouth. "I'm not going to kill you yet, for I may find that I can use you later on for a certain purpose. Raising the staff the Emperor struck Troy in the head. "Sleep tight, I will be back for you in a while." Keeping his glowing red eyes on Troy, he turned and left the room locking the door behind him.

Seeing the black mass leaving the room Troy slowly crawled to where the Piratain Emperor had stood near the computer consul. Reacting underneath he tried to get to the medallion. The stabbing pain roared through his head, giving up on the medallion, Troy laid back against the computer. He's fighting to keep his mind alert.

"Computer, He was saying in a low voice, before the blackness started swirling around his head and the dizziness came as if her was on a ferrous wheel. "Lock out the Piratain Emperors voice mode and all of his access codes on the main terminal."

"PIRATAIN EMPEROR'S VOICE MODE AND ACCESS CODES ARE NOW LOCKED."

"Thanks" his mind was edging towards darkness and he thought that he heard the computer say welcome.

The Emperor went looking for his lieutenant to see if everything is powered down since the star child had taken the medallions out of the device, now the Emperor had to devise another plan to get Elura to surrender and to bow down to there new leader. Pride and hate swelled up in side of him as he walked the silent halls. Entering the control center he saw how empty it was, the screams of rage came from the Emperor piercing the empty room as sounds echoed of the walls. He suddenly knew what he had done by drawing on the others had released them from his control. He walks fast towards the consul.

"Computer, where are the others of my staff?" He entered the access code.

"CAN NOT COMPLY, ACCESS CODE IS INVALID." He hits the consul with his fist.

"Who requested it?"

"THE HUMAN REQUESTED IT." The Emperor fumed and knew Troy had closed him out of the computer.

"Override his commands!" He yelled at the computer.

"CAN NOT COMPLY ALL ACCESS CODES HAVE BEEN LOCKED OUT.

"Override his commands, or I will pull your circuits and override them myself."

"CAN NOT COMPLY ALL ACCESS CODES HAVE BEEN LOCKED OUT." The emperor listened and then he went to a panel pulling it off and exposing the circuit board, studying the board he located the off switch. Reaching inside he was shocked and stunned for the computer was protecting itself with a force field. Pulling back quickly, so he would not to get shocked again. Going to the other end of the consul he did the same locating the panel and ripped it of in frustration and saw the force field surrounding the circuitry.

"You think that you can out wit me!" He yelled the insult at the computer. Standing there he scanned the room with his eyes and finding what he was looking for and went to grab his staff and quickly went over the consul raising his staff he struck the consul and immediately folded up into the wall as is it was in pain and didn't wish to be inflicted upon again. The Emperor exploded with all the rage anger and hate. He destroyed anything in his path of destruction. His form began to change once more and the blackness seems to look like a deep void of endless blackness to which nothing can escape it. After a while he returned to his former himself. He saw the destruction that he had caused in the control center. Chairs ribbed way from the floor and the consul to the navigation systems took quite a beating and the streams of curtains were pulled from there holding place. Feeling the strain of his terrible anger the Emperor turned a way and went to his room to rest. Thinking sleep is the only solution for right now. Hoping that he will feel better and thinking rationally. Punching a side pane and a door slides open he went into the room as the door closes behind him.

CHAPTER SIXTEEN

As the sun shown brightly inside the room, Faith squint her eyes from the sun light. Sitting up in the bed she rubbed the sleep from her eyes.

Looking around the room wondering where she was, after a few minutes it all came back to her. Quickly pulling back the blanket she got up. Realizing she still had her clothes on. Startled as the bed folded itself up, and back into the wall, wondering if the Imperial Council meeting went ok and that Troy or Tommy had came back yet since she was to busy with helping those who were coming in from the portal Tommy and Troy had created. All she knew was what those who were there to witness some of it told her. Leaving the room she met Alan, he was on his way to see her.

"Good morning!" He chimed in with a smile.

"Good morning to you as well." she said, still trying to wake up wishing she had a cup of coffee right about now. Running her fingers through her hair, just imagining what she looked like to him. "Have you found out anything new about Troy and Tommy?" Alan stopped short of her thinking about it.

"NO, nothing more than you know." Faith took a hold of Alan's arm and then smiled at him.

"Well let's go see the Emperor and Empress, maybe they know what is going on. For it has been a long time since we heard from them."

"Okay, I'm game lets go." He gave her a kiss as they walked down the hall. Entering the Central Command Post they saw no one, for it was clear of all life?

"Computer, where is both the Emperor and Empress?" Faith asked. Feeling that something was not right in the air she could not shake the feeling that something was terribly wrong, but told herself that her mind has been working over time lately.

"THEY ARE IN THEIR ROOM."

"Where is that?" Immediately a hologram map appeared in front of them, showing them the way. Studying the map she found it difficult to follow. "Well can you tell them that Alan and Faith need to talk to them?" Said Alan for he also found it hard to follow it. Ever since they arrived on Elura they couldn't find it, not unless some one took them there. For the place was like a maze, you can easily get lost in it.

"AFFRIMATIVE"

It had only been a split second as the Emperor and Empress were standing in front of them. Neither one of them spoke at all, but Faith saw it in their face what they were about to say was not good news. Alan could not stand the silence any longer.

"What's wrong, why isn't there anyone here working to save Tommy and Troy or even monitoring their life signs?" The Emperor looked sadly at them.

"Right after you both left to get some rest last night." stopping for he could not look them in the eyes for the grief he felt was too much for him too bare. "We found Tommy's and Troy' life signs had disappeared off' of our monitors." Faith felt num allover and in a sudden shock over the news she just heard. Deep down inside she knew that Tommy and Troy were still alive and refused to accept this nonsense. Taking Alan's hand in hers hoping to find comfort there, but instead she found herself thinking with fear and hopelessness. Afraid to turn her eyes to meet his for she knew she'd fine the same fear there."

"There got to be something we can do to get Tommy and Troy back?" He said. He pleaded with the Emperor and Empress. Alan shook his head thinking how unfair this was.

"Nothing can be done at this time, for if we transport anyone over there then we become open to an attack and that means taking a risk of being detected by his computers. Not to mention the fact that he maybe using them both to lure us in a trap, knowing that we will come for him. These are the options we already took in consideration." Alan could no longer stand it. Allowing what the Emperor said to go in one ear and out the other. He knew that he could not even think of leaving Tommy and Troy on that ship to die, because of lack of control and understanding.

"Well," said Alan flatly. "If you are not willing to take risks then, I will use the medallion since being here I've learned how to use it, I'm not going to stand around here and watch my friends die." Looking at Faith who seemed to be only half listening to what they were talking about. Alan took a hold of her hand, giving it a gentle squeeze she immediately snapped back to there present conversation.

"Yes," Faith said dully. "We will use them if we have to." The Empress shook her head, looking down to the floor in defeat.

"Well, it seems that we have no other choice but to let both of you go on your quest rather we like it or not. Since you are a guest here on our planet we must at least try to protect you while you are on your journey. If anything happens to your life signs we will immediately transport you both out of there unless you tell us through any means of communication." She lifted her head to show them that she met business. "Fair enough"

"Yes, it's fair enough." Said Alan, satisfied with the decision that was made he and Faith walked away to make plans for their quest. Watching them go the Empress gave orders to have both Alan's and Faith's life signs monitored. She looked at her husband.

"You know humans can be irrational as well as they can be pleasant people." The Emperor chuckled at her remark. Wrapping her arms around herself as if the air around her just got cold but she knew that it was the feeling of danger that both of them were going to face. Deep in thought she didn't hear her husband's reply to her remark. Still looking at the direction that Faith and Alan went even though they were no longer in sight.

"My Love, are you all right." He said with a concern note in his voice. Looking at her face he knew that her mind was on their two guests. "Don't worry they will be fine." She looked at him.

"Its not that I'm worried about them, well it's just this feeling I have, like there is something terribly wrong here. I mean a feeling of uncertainty, I guess for I can place it."

"Your just worried that is all." The Emperor said not giving it anymore thought for he felt the same way and he didn't want the Empress to worry anymore than she already is. As they walked outside of the Central Command Post they were both smiling and enjoying each others company for the first time since the humans arrived. Their thoughts were on each other and on the hope that their son Tommy was still alive. As Alan sat in the chair in the Imperial conference chamber going over their plan to rescue Troy Beckman and Tommy was still alive. He turned to Faith to see what she thought about what was laid out on the table in front of her.

"I don't know this sounds kind of risky." She said with uncertainty.

"Well it is the only way we've got, and if we get caught then at least we did the best we can to help them I really see no other way." He shrugged his shoulders.

"By taking on the Piratain Emperor ourselves, that's suicide getting our selves killed will not help these people one bit."

She stood up in defense.

"I know that, if you don't want to go then I suggest that you stay here on Elura where you will be safe. I don't want you to go anyway." Alan said without looking at her afraid that if he did she would see how frighten he was for her.

"Forget about leaving me behind because I'm going rather you like it or not." Putting her hands on her hips and narrowing the slits in her eyes to show him that she met business.

"Okay, okay I give up you can go."" He threw his hands up as to block the accusation of wanting to leave her behind.

"Now since that is settled is there anything else we need to disgust before we embark on our mission together." Sitting back into her chair she could not belief that her just had her first argument and won. She smiled at Alan, wondering if he was thinking the same thing at the moment. Putting aside all her fears and doubts about the mission she concentrates on listening to him carefully so that she would know what to do if the situation ever got the best of both of them. After awhile an Imperial Servant came into the room with a tray full of fruit and a second servant brought a picture of water with two glasses on the tray.

"Excuse me you both need to eat and to be strengthen for your mission as you will call it." Bowing to them he left the room so to let them eat in peace.

"Well that is about it, but I can't promise that it will go as planed. We just have to make the best of our situations when we cross them." Alan said as he got up and went to the other side of the table. Picking up a glass he began to pour some water and grabbed some fruit he ate. Still sitting in her seat Faith looked at Alan as he ate, not really hungry she made herself eat. As they ate the fruit and drank the water the Emperor and Empress came into the Imperial Chamber and behind them was an Imperial Servant hold a box. Both Faith and Alan got up from the table out of respect for royalty.

"Oh, please both of you sit and eat." She waved them down to sit. "How do you like our fruits?"

"It is remarkable; I have not tasted anything this good on Earth." Said Alan as he took another bite of what he thought was an apple but it tasted watery and sweet.

"Uh, these grapes are very good they taste like sweet and sour put together." Faith said as she was talking with her mouth full, she thought that she was not hungry and now it is like she can't get enough.

"I am glad that you like them we take pride in our fruit and vegetables nothing but the very best for all." The Imperial Servant went to the table and sat the box down opening its lid she bowed to Faith and Alan and then turned and did the same to Emperor and Empress. Then she left the chamber so that they will be able to talk in private. Upon seeing the medallion both Alan and Faith stopped eating and turned to the Emperor and Empress with questions in there eyes.

"This is my brother's medallion, we forgot that Tommy was not wearing one when he was captured and thought it would be better if Troy would have it so that Tommy would have his back. We had it reprogrammed and with Troy's DNA in it as well." Said the Emperor he went to the box as if he wanted to touch it to remember to good times.

"I never thought that you had a brother is he here, how come we have not met him can he help us out with our predicament?" Faith said.

"No, he is not here and will not be able to help." Empress said in a low voice.

"Did he die?" Alan asked

"No, he is alive and you have met him." Alan was racking his brain trying to remember who he was but came up empty.

"I'm sorry I thought that you said we have met him, but I can't seem to remember what he looks like." Faith asked first for she was thinking the same thing.

"You have met him." The Emperor voice sounded cracked. "He is the Piratain Emperor."

"What!" Both Alan and Faith said at the same time.

"You see my brother got greedy and wanted the throne for himself and would do anything to get it. Including murder his whole family. This was made known to the Council by the prophets at that time. They became distraught for they have to judge one of our own people for the very first time. They had him imprisoned inside the mountain in the north to keep him away from the population but still the quarreling and bickering began soon the people demanded him to be freed. So they let him go hoping that the decease would die down, but it did not. Soon the people were changing their form was being altered into a grotesque creatures and it was spreading fast the prophets told the council that they had to be taken off this planet. So the Council gathered them and past judgment on them finding them guilty the sentence was banishment for the planet never to return. The ships were created and put them in and blasted them into space on autopilot. Believe me there were hundreds of them and we lost them all because what my brother had done. Until twelve of your earth years ago they return to seek out their revenge on the planet, But they came in disguise tricking the people thinking that they were tech traders, well that part was made up to protect the people from the real reason. And now we have been paying for it. The time to stop is here. The Emperor had finished.

"So this is all about wanting the control and to enslave your people right." The Empress slowly nods. "So why didn't you kill him when you had the chance to do so?"

"Our species can not kill Alan, never, if we do we will be condemning ourselves to being just like him and that just can't happen." The Emperor walked over the other side of the chamber avoiding eye contact.

"I am sorry; I just can not imagine how difficult this is for you suppressing a side of your self just to live a normal as possible life. It must indeed be very hard on you and your people.

"On the contrary, my people had been living happier and have seen great things happened. The hate the greed the lies all of it is a danger to us because it changes us outwardly. For your species it changes the inside and your actions you're able to dim it out of your lives, and go on living." Alan listened to the Emperor.

"That is true for us and how we and your people are different from us. We also were taught things at a young age to love or hate to be told what to do and say. As we get older we see the difference and choose what path we want to walk and live on." Alan said and Faith was there nodding her head in agreement with him.

"What about your quest have you found out what you are going to do?" asked The Emperor glad to be away from the gloomy conversation.

"Yes, we have decided to create a portal in the throne room for that is where we last saw Tommy and Troy. If they are not there then, we will search the ship until we do or they find us." Faith said for she had remembered it word from word.

"What if you come up against the Piratain Emperor?" Said the Empress as she looked down and the plans Alan had created.

"Then we will use the medallion again him." Alan said with confidence they will win the round.

"When and where are you planning to do this?" The Emperor came back to the table to see the plan Alan made up.

"Well in just a few minutes and where we will do it is in the Central Command Post." Alan told them as he started rolling up the plans and Faith got up from her chair and pick up the box that contained Troy's medallion she was feeling a little bit anxious and wanted to get this over with.

"By the way, was that what the Imperial Council wanted to talk about?" She asked

"Yes," Said the Empress "and something else was discussed."

"What was it" Faith said.

"You all will find out later after this war is over." The Empress winked at her husband as he smiled a little. "May we accompany you to the Central Command Post?"

"Sure we would like that your majesty." Alan said with great respect for the people of Elura.

They entered the Central Command Post and saw that it was pact with the people of Elura and some of their own as well. It got quite real quick as they made their way to the center of the room. As they went the people were bowing to them as well as to the Emperor and Empress. The same little boy who had found his mother was now standing on the table he smiled at Alan as the approached the table he puts the plans on it. Some of the people were shouting encouragement to them as they enter the center of the room. Alan wave a hand at them and then realized that his face was wet with tears streaming down his face Faith took his hand and gave it a gentle squeeze he turned to her saw that she too was crying and smiling at the same time. Letting go of her hand he brought out the medallion and held it in his hands he brought it up above his head closing his eyes he concentrated on the image of the throne room on the ship. Feeling the air charge up around him and the medallion was warm in his hands. He allowed the patience to fill him like a warm summer day. As the medallion got brighter and he then saw a bright flash of light behind his eyes lids He heard the Empress on his other side of him.

"Open your eyes Alan and see what you have created." He opened them and saw the portal big and round like that of water. Faith stepped forwarded and went through then he did the same looking back he saw the portal had closed from behind.

CHAPTER SEVENTEEN

Darkness engulfs Troy sending him spiraling downward to a bottomless pit which seems to have no end echoes of the past came barreling in voice to loud to distinguish as they all were melding together to become the ultimate voice that was the loudest. A scene takes form Troy knew which nightmares he was to face for it is the one he had faced many times. Somehow this seems different clearer and very detailed. Standing there letting the dream to unfold watching his partner being killed by a boy who was a little older that Tommy by one or two years. The monster appears killing the boy out of blinding rage. The boy falls and slums over, the creature turns to Troy.

"I do not want to do fight you again it is pointless. He stood his ground in hopes that he wouldn't have to repeat his own demise with the creature.

"Then let's not fight, instead come to me and embrace me forgive me for my actions." Without neither hesitation nor fear Troy went forward in love had embraced the bulky creature who in retuned wrapped his own arms around him. As they hugged not letting go Troy felt the creatures form change getting smaller his heart came lighter and the strength that had grown within him. Pulling away there stood Tommy eyes gleaming bright blue, the nightmare dream scene had changed into a beautiful meadow the sound of birds rushing water falls a slight breeze as they both basket in the warmth of the sunrays. He bent down to his knees so to be eye to eye with him.

"How is this possible?" he asked him.

"Our minds have always been linked together from the very start, which was how I knew that you were special. You now have a reservoir of untapped power with in you. Now that you have taken the final step against the darkness and you have choose to love and forgive yourself for you own faults and failures." Troy cut him off.

"Okay kiddo, rub it in." Grabbing Tommy's nose and shook it about playfully. Tommy giggles.

"I like that, Mason used to call me kiddo too. I sure miss her you would have liked her." Troy recall Masons file and agreed with him that he would have liked Mason.

"Tommy what do you mean that I had untapped power?"

"You're like me, a star child except you are from Earth. That is why I was so over whelmed in seeing you that day I gave you the medallion I knew that it was safe with you. It was the feeling which caught me by surprise a kinship feeling like that of family." Troy eyes welled up with tears for it was the same he felt with Tommy. Tears ran down his face as he felt every drop.

"I have been feeling the same way and I could not forget it, you have helped me change in ways I thought would never be repaired. To have a life again with out the grim memories hanging over my head each day to me that was no life at all."

"Yeah, it was the same with me when I was going to school and having the accident of the death of my parents going with me form day to day, so I know how you feel." His eyes searched to meadows in wanting to run through them.

"If you are here with me that would mean you are still alive!" He shouted.

"Of course I am alive," The boy smiled.

"But the Piratain Emperor said that you were dead and it sure looked that way before he beat me to a pulp." Tommy eyes widen in shock.

"Then you have to wake up and get the medallion around my neck, it has healing properties." Tommy shouted for him to wake up, shaking him saying it over and over until the voice changed, it was that of a woman's and a man's voice.

"Troy wake up man common wake up." Feeling the shaking Troy opened his eyes at first they are blurry, as they started to clear he saw both Alan Tate and Faith McCray. Slowly getting up he began to feel the pain coming back into his body.

"The medallion where is it?" Faith was surprised he knew that she was carrying one that was for him. Opening the box she gave him the medallion. Was the question she wanted answer, instead he held up a finger, putting it around his neck and not saying anything he concentrated on the floor he stretched out is hand as they heard something scraping on the floor and flew into Troy's hand. Quickly he turned to Tommy's body and put the medallion over his head and waited on his chest both his and Tommy's was glowing dark blue and hummed throughout the body. Troy felt the pain lessening. He heard both Alan and Faith gasp in surprise and were amazed at what they can do for Troy whole face was swollen barely recognizable and at that time they were seeing his features again. He looked as if nothing happened to him, but they saw that he was somehow changed.

"Why isn't Tommy waking up?" Faith said as the dark blue color was getting lighter.

"Faith get on the other side of Tommy, Alan stays on this side of him and I will be at his feet." Quickly he took off his medallion placing it flat in both hands. "Bring forth Love!" He commanded the medallion left his hands and attached itself to Tommy's medallion. He looked at Alan and encouraged him to do the same. Understanding what Troy was asking of him. Taking his medallion from around his neck he placed it flat in both hands.

"Bring forth Patience!" Alan's medallion did the same as it attaches to Tommy's. Faith quickly did the same.

"Bring forth Joy! She commanded and the medallion left her hands and attaches it self once more. The waited but nothing happened then Tommy eyes opened slowly. In a low whisper they could barely hear.

"Bring forth Self-Control." As he said those words all four medallions glowed fiercely creating a shield about Tommy as the medallion changed different colors. Tommy's red, Troy's blue, Faith's orange and Alan's purple. It had intensified to the point they were disappearing on by one returning to the owner's neck forming a suit around their bodies as if the medallion were alive according it the color's it had displayed each one different and in other way with different abilities for the wearer. Tommy stood there in front of them all completely healed and smiling from ear to ear and ran to hug all of them for he has missed them. As they chattered and forgetting all about the Piratain Emperor was standing inside the room.

"Oh, happy reunions, oh how I love them. They make me sick!" He yelled with contentment in his voice. All four of them were startled by the appearance of the Piratain Emperor for they forgot where they were.

"We are not here to fight you, just came for Tommy and Troy and then you can go on your way." Faith announced.

"I will go on my way alright, straight to Earth, I hear that it needs to be conquered. I am just the kind of guy to do it." He snickered.

"Then we have a problem, you see we will not let you go any where except to sleep forever, sounds good to you?" Troy mocked him. They heard the growl coming from the Piratains throat, his eyes glowing red. "Now, now play nice if you look around you'll see it is four again one, that is not a fair battle, well given your size maybe it is."

"Don't enrage him Troy, for we do not know the limit of his power, much less our own?" Alan said.

"Okay I won't but am not leaving here so he can get his greedy hands on Earth." Troy folded his arms.

"He's not going to." Tommy spoke up. "He's powerless and he knows it, or we would be lying flat on the floor by now." All eyes turned to Tommy. "Uncle it is over, revert back and be done with all the rage and hate and hostility it sounds exhausting I know that it must feel like that too. I am sure that mother and father would have missed you if they were alive."

"I was told that all those who had reverted back to their natural state do not remember what they did or who they were before. Perhaps the same thing will happen to you if you are willing." The Piratain Emperor sat down on the floor, defeated and alone.

"That will not happen to me I am the source of the disease which is why those who were affected were banished with me. I do not know how it was started a sting of jealousy or greed I don't know. I thing the best thing for me is to die so that I will never hurt another race or planet I am tired of all these feelings they are exhausting. How did I manage to let it get this far is beyond me." He turned to Troy his eyes on longer glowing in rage but sad and empty. "Do what you must to ensure that I would never do this again." Tommy came over to him as the others tried to keep him away. He took a hold of a big finger.

"Perhaps I was quick to judge you. You are after all part of my family and families stick together." Tears of shame and humiliation mixed with fear of the unknown came from the Piratains as he engulfed his nephews hand in his.

"THERE IS AN UNAUTHERIZED PERSON ON BOARD I REPEAT AN UNAUTHERIZED PERSON ON BOARD." Show me said Troy walking to the consul. The screen displayed a person coming out of the shadows. Tommy looked hard but could not make it out.

"Can you magnify image please?" the screen was bigger and the image more indefinable. "Oh no," He said in a low voice.

"What is Tommy?" Faith said

"That is Kevin, I was told that he was killed and some how he seem different some how." The Piratain Emperor looked up into the screen.

"He looks like I did when I started changing, and it took one to two year before the transformation was completed." Troy turned to the Piratain Emperor.

"Did it take the others that long too?" He shook his head.

"No, theirs was fast and was transformed with in a day at the most sometimes it was sooner. For the looks of it I say that Kevin has been brewing for about a year maybe more."

"How can that be I have been with him for about three months and he did not look like that?" He looked at Faith for confirmation

"That is correct Tommy, I have not seen him like this neither." The Piratain shifted his weight around.

"Was he wearing a medallion?" Tommy looked at his Uncle.

"Yes, He said that I gave it to him when I was younger, because I had chosen him to be my Imperial Guardian." The Piratain shook head immediately upon hearing that.

"That was a lie he had told you, that was never in our customs for a royal child to choose his Imperial Guardian or have a medallion given to him." He looked at Troy. "May I have control back for at least a minute or two and then you can close me back out again?" He nodded his in approval.

"Computer, release the Piratain Emperors access codes."

"PIRATAIN EMPERORS ACCESS CODES ARE RELAESED."

"Computer, scan for a medallion on the intruder?" Piratain Emperor said.

"I AM SCANNING INTRUDER NOW." As the computer was working silence fell over them as they saw an imprint of a medallion with a green background and the imprint and the city of Elura.

"Hey, that is the medallion I had seen on Kevin." They all agreed for the exception of the Piratain Emperor, who fell back even more again the wall in despair of the news he had just seen.

"Just as I thought, the medallion that he is wearing belongs to my father your grandfather Tommy. He was murdered and they could never find his medallion they thought that I had killed him. I never could I love my father very much despite my difference between me and my brother. If want confirmation I suggest you use a secure channel." Troy did just that and before long the Elurain Emperor was on the screen.

"Troy good to see everyone is okay!" He shouted.

"Yes Emperor we are, but the reason we are contacting you now is that we found Kevin we want to know if you or anyone has given him a medallion?"

"No, Imperial Servant doses not get a medallion they are for royal family members and social guests such as for self."

"Did you send him on the mission to retrieve Tommy and us?"

"Yes, and gave him three medallions, poor Mason was kill in the retrieval and we have her medallion here in its case. What's up with the questions?"

"Kevin has a medallion which looks green in the background and an Elurain city in the foreground."

"That sounds like my fathers medallion, we thought that my brother had murdered him and taken the medallion."

"That is enough on the accusation father, we know that Uncle did not do it and yet he was blamed for it." A light suddenly turned on in Tommy's head. He turned to the Piratain Emperor. "Have you ever seen him for before today?"

"Yes, he was serving as a royal servant in those days. He was younger, I say about fifteen Earth years." The Elurain Emperor jumped in.

"Yes, I remember he liked working in fathers gardens." The Piratains Emperors head pops with excitement.

"Which means he could be the one who killed father, if that is true." The Elurain Emperor finished the sentence

"He could be the first one to become infected and that he is the carrier. But that is crazy he has been here since your banishment and after that there was no more infected Elurains."

"Could it be that he has found a way to control it?" Tommy said.

"It is possible son, that Kevin has been fooling all of us. We won't know until we ask him."

"Computer, where is the intruder?"

"HE IS ON HIS WAY TO THE THRONE ROOM." The Piratain Emperor seems to be getting smaller and less bulky. For he was able to get up and move from the door he hid behind a bulky generator so that Kevin would not know that he was there. Kevin enters running like a scared little kid. All four of them turned to him not amused by his attempts to pull the wool over their eyes.

"Where were you, we thought that you were dead?" Tommy came straight out with it. Kevin changed to the handsome hologram man.

"It was a cool trick I did it was the Piratain Emperor though he killed me, I sure fooled him." He smiled. Tommy continued to question him.

"Where did you get the medallion Kevin?" he giggled a little.

"Nice one, you know that you gave it to me." Tommy's face drew a blank so that Kevin wouldn't see that he knew that truth.

"Well according to my father and mother, there is no such customs on our planet. Just curious how did you manipulate my mother hologram processor to get her to say those things, for me believe it all?" Kevin saw no reason to continue with the charade. So he took his true from.

"No, I created my own." He smiles.

"Where did you get the medallion?" Tommy folded his arms not enjoy this for Kevin was to be his friend.

"I was working for your old grandfather always telling me where to go what to do and who I can see until I could not stand it any more so I grabbed a heave stick and beat him until he was no longer breathing, so I saw the chance to take the medallion at first I did not know what it can do. Then I realized what I had it was power, when your father saw your brother stand over him with the stick in his hand like a stupid fool he was and then I leaked a rumor that he was trying to kill your father and that was all I had to do to wage a royal war. After your Uncle was banished I found I could turn Elurains into Piratains just by touching them that is why there were so many that went with him."

"Did you do all this just to cover up the murder of my grandfather?" Tommy shouted at him.

"No, I did it because I enjoyed it; I feed on it and savored it." Kevin smile so big it looked as if his mouth was going to split. Faith steps forwards strain from the impulse to slap Kevin silly.

"You make me sick, to make me think that you were so innocent that I actually cared about you." Kevin looked surprised at what she said to him. As if Faith had dumped hot water on him. He looks at her hard and she went flying up and suspended in midair.

"It was a shame after all I did for you I got Robert Loudon to like you and if you ask me he was obsessed with you." Laughing he turned to Tommy. "You thought that I was nothing more than a brat before I showed you my true face, Oh boy you ate it right up." He giggled hard for a time. But the best one was when the Elurain Emperor thought that his brother killed their father.

"That is enough!" A thunderous resounds in the room. And the Piratain Emperor stood ready to fight. "Let her go!" His deep voice growled. Kevin Smiled.

"That will be my pleasure?" He bowed to the Piratain Emperor. "Your majesty" As he let Faith go she fell and Alan had caught her. Troy took the opportunity concentrating he ripped Kevin's medallion off his neck and sent it to the Piratain Emperor who had put it on and immediately his from began to change back to himself for he was no longer Piratain but Elurain. Tommy ran to his Uncle and hugged him for it was all he wanted to do since he arrived.

"No my medallion, give it back!" His form got bigger and bulkier really fast.

"Computer, contain the intruder." "Immediately a force field went up with some kind of chemical being disbursed with it is as Kevin slowly went down and was out like a light.

"THE INTRUDER IS CONTAINED." Troy mouths the words thank you. "YOU'RE WELCOME" Everyone laughed lightly.

"We need a plan in what to do with Kevin?" Tommy steps forward.

"Well, I tell you what we are not going to suggest is death." Troy puts a hand on the boy.

"That is right we are not going to suggest that, But I do have on suggestion. That is or leave him hear on the ship and allow the ship to be on auto pilot shutting Kevin out of it commands subroutine. And let it fly way out loosing all it star charts along the way so that Kevin will never again hurt anyone else ever again and to send out a beacon warning other ships to stay away for it was contained with an unknown disease.

"That is an excellent idea said the Elurain Emperor said. "Do it and fast. Now I would like to speak to my brother alone please." Every one follow behind Troy and Kevin was transported to a confined cell until things are done and they are off the ship.

It had taken awhile and Troy checked things over so to make sure that there would be no way for Kevin to gain control of the ship for a long, long time. Now they were ready to be transported of the ship and the Tommy's Uncle gave one last look around he was ready to leave this part of his life behind him and to move on restoring his relationship with his family and his people. Tommy came and stood right beside him.

"Uncle, let us go home." The both took their positions on the platform.

"Computer, give us five minutes and then start your command and subroutines."

"AFFRIMATIVE, GOODBYE TROY BECKMAN."

"Goodbye computer." The transporters just became active and then they were gone.

CHAPTER EIGHTEEN

As they materialize in the Central Command Post there were cheers and a big celebration was underway for this marks they end of their war which was waged for twelve Earth years And that their Prophecy came true it was later discovered that their was indeed two star child not one. Also The Emperor's brother was restored in the royal family and that they had a lot of catching up to do. Alan Tate and Faith McCray had asked if they can call Elura their home for they wanted to live in a peaceful non-violent world so that they can raise a family once they were married which according to Faith would not be anytime soon. For now they wanted to enjoy their new citizenship as Elurains. The Emperor and Empress Shali were finally given their bodies back although being frozen for Twelve Years is going to get on use to the feeling and new experiences together. The Elurains had already sent two vessels to Earth returning those who were taken and their minds had been altered to protect Elura and to help them to keep their insanity intact for who on Earth would believe in on life on other planets. If you were to tell me before all this had happened I would have said that you were nuts.

Well my final day has arrived and it was time to go back to Earth with my memories intact, for I do not want to forget one thing that has been to me.

The Empress entered the room just as I had finished my entry in my journal.

"Troy, do you have some time before you departure?" She asked rubbing her hands together she still trying to get use to it and to her surrounding.

"Sure, I am all yours Empress." Grabbing Troy off the chair they walked fast.

"Good, walk with me to the Central Command Post." Troy let out a soft laugh for he had enjoyed ever minute with Tommy's parents For the hardest thing he will do is to say good bye to Tommy for he sees him as family no longer just a boy but a son he will be proud of having. They went through the sliding door and into the Centurial Command Post where practically the whole city was their. As they made it up to the platform one of the Imperial Council Member was standing before him. The Empress let go of Troy and took her place beside her husband and brother in law. Tommy was stand next to his mother.

"Troy Beckman" Said the Imperial Council in a loud voice so that all could hear them. "On your knees please." He asks. Troy obeyed him and looks up in the Elurains face held no information as to what the heck was going on so he decided to go with it. "I hear by bestow upon you the royal title of prince; you will be expected to uphold our laws and the royal decisions that are made within the royal court. If you accept this and where ever you may be you will be Prince Troy Beckman weather you are on Earth or Elura." The Emperor and Empress smiled and Tommy's Uncle nodded in approval then Troy's eyes met Tommy's who was beaming from head to toe. He turned the other way to see Faith and Alan smiling. He looked straight ahead again with the Imperial Council Member in front of him.

"Yes, I accept the title of Prince." The crowd cheered and clapped their hands

"Then I crown you with wisdom. And give in one hand loyalty and in the other love. About your neck the royal seal made just for you." The Imperial Council member turned the medallion about so that Troy could see nothing in the background but silver and in the foreground what the royal family of five for he was included. "This medallion will serve you and guide you and must be worn at all times. Another Imperial Council Member stood behind him lifting the medallion he still worn and was replaced with the royal one. Both Imperial Council Members pick him off the platform and on his feet they both turned him to face the crowd. One of them announced him to the crowd.

"I give you your newest Prince Troy Beckman!"

"Hail Prince Troy Beckman, Hail Prince Troy Beckman." The crowed said as the cheered and clapped their hands. Troy saw indeed smiling and waving his hands and found his cheeks were wet with tears of joy. The royal family surrounded him and hugged him welcoming him in their family. Alan and Faith came up and congratulated him. They were dressed in fine clothing. Feeling Tommy hugging him he bent down giving him a kiss on the forehead he retuned his hug.

It was decided the Tommy will go and live with Troy as his Earth Father and when they return he will be Tommy Guardian Father if anything should happen to the Emperor and Empress he will inherit Tommy as his son and with all the duties of running Elura will be shared with his new brother.

Three months have past and Tommy was doing quite will in making new friend as Troy left the house he saw Tommy throwing a football around with his new friends from his school. He wave to Tommy as he got into the car and drove to his new job at the F.B.I when he got back he filled out an incident report explaining his where bouts and left out the story of Elura. He had Sheriff Wilson backing him up all the way. The board was impressed that they decided to promote Troy and was told to take the file he had written out with him. He entered the building all eyes where on him as he made his way to the receptionist desk.

"May I help you?" she said.

"I'm Agent Troy Beckman." She Stop what she was doing.

"Oh, I am sorry Agent Beckman we have been expecting you. Your office it just around the corner here with a glass door." She Smile and got up and showed him to his new office. On the Door was.

AGENT TROY BECKMAN
DIERCTOR OF OPERATIONS OF THE UNEXPLAINED

He saw how big the office was he would have to bring his office furniture to fill the space with. He turns to the receptionist.

"Where do I turn in finished case files?"

"That will be on level down, would you like me to send it down there for you?" She said nicely.

"No, thank you Mrs." He didn't' know her name.

"It's Miss Burlington and I am your receptionist." She smiled and went back to her desk. Closing the door and went to the elevator and pressed the down the elevator he gets in and was on his way down. Getting out of the small elevator he went down a hallway where there was a security guard sitting at a small cramped desk.

"Sign in here please." Giving the clipboard to Troy he singed his name and shows his badge to the guard. Allowing him to pass opening the next door into a room with files upon files and rows of rows of nothing but case files. Taking his file to the desk across the room where a man who sat behind a desk typing away.

"What can I do for you Agent?" He droned as he continues to type.

"Yes, I have a case closed file that is finished." The picking of the typewriter stopped as the man looked at him kind of funny.

"What is there something on my face or something on my tie?"

"No, sorry it is just that we have not had a closed file before."

"What are all of these he waves his free hand to?"

"They are all unsolved cases dating back to the nineteen forties.

"Wow that is a lot to go through." Troy could not believe it.

"So, what do you do?" The man asked.

"I am Director of Operation of the Unexplained." The man snapped up

"Agent Beckman we were expecting you." Standing to his feet and took his file from and place it on and empty rack. "Our first case wrapped up in decays." He smiled at him. He stuck out his hand and shook Troy's. "Good luck, and welcome to hell you are going to need it. Troy looked at the rows upon rows of files........